THE MAGNIFICENT MARRIAGE

Lady Dorinda Burne had always led a retiring life
—a disfiguring skin complaint made her feel uncomfortable in company. But now she was chaper-
oning her sister to Singapore where Lettice would
marry the fabulously rich, brilliantly clever Maximus Kirby. Dorinda found that she admired him
more than any man she had ever met and in his
presence always felt at a loss for words. But
Dorinda was about to encounter perils far more
fearsome than facing Maximus Kirby. Yet, awaiting her too was a magnificent love and a new life
more beautiful than any she had ever imagined.

BARBARA CARTLAND

Books by BARBARA CARTLAND

Romantic Novels

*The Daring Deception (#1)
*No Darkness for Love (#2)
*The Little Adventure (#3)
*Lessons in Love (#4)
*Journey to Paradise (#5)
*The Bored Bridegroom (#6)
*The Penniless Peer (#7)

*The Dangerous Dandy (#8)
*The Ruthless Rake (#9)
*The Wicked Marquis (#10)
*The Castle of Fear (#11)
*The Glittering Lights (#12)
*A Sword to the Heart (#13)
*The Karma of Love (#14)
*The Magnificent Marriage (#15)

Autobiographical and Biographical

The Isthmus Years 1919–1939
The Years of Opportunity 1939–1945
I Search for Rainbows 1945–1966
We Danced All Night 1919–1929
Ronald Cartland
    (with a Foreword by Sir Winston Churchill)
Polly, My Wonderful Mother

Historical

Bewitching Women
The Outrageous Queen
    (The Story of Queen Christina of Sweden)
The Scandalous Life of King Carol
The Private Life of King Charles II
The Private Life of Elizabeth, Empress of Austria
Josephine, Empress of France
Diane de Poitiers
Metternich—the Passionate Diplomat

Sociology

You in the Home
The Fascinating Forties
Marriage for Moderns
Be Vivid, Be Vital
Love, Life and Sex
Look Lovely, Be Lovely
Vitamins for Vitality
Husbands and Wives

Etiquette
The Many Facets of Love
Sex and the Teenager
The Book of Charm
Living Together
Woman—The Enigma
The Youth Secret
The Magic of Honey

Barbara Cartland's Health Food Cookery Book
Barbara Cartland's Book of Beauty and Health
Men Are Wonderful

*Published by Bantam Books

The Magnificent Marriage

BARBARA CARTLAND

THE MAGNIFICENT MARRIAGE
A Bantam Book / February 1975

Published simultaneously in the United States and Canada

Bantam Books are published by Bantam Books, Inc. Its trade-
mark, consisting of the words "Bantam Books" and the por-
trayal of a bantam, is registered in the United States Patent
Office and in other countries. Marca Registrada. Bantam
Books, Inc., 666 Fifth Avenue, New York, New York 10019.

PRINTED IN THE UNITED STATES OF AMERICA

Author's Note

It is a medical fact that eczema can disappear in the warm, moist climate of South Asia. I myself have seen it happen overnight in Singapore and Bangkok.

While Maximus Kirby and Dorinda are imaginary characters, the background of Singapore is completely factual and part of its history, including the description of the pirates. Snake bites were treated in the manner described both in England and abroad up to twenty-five years ago.

Chapter One

1879

The Earl of Alderburne looked up from the letter he was holding in his hand with an expression of delight in his eyes.

"It has come, Elizabeth!" he exclaimed.

The Countess, seated at the other end of the breakfast table, glanced at him in surprise.

"What has?" she enquired.

"The letter from Kirby. Dammit all, you know I have been expecting it for weeks!"

"Yes, of course, Hugo, and very disagreeable it has made you! What does he say?"

The Earl consulted the letter once again, and there was no doubt he was delighted with every word he read. Finally he said:

"He asks that Letty should travel to Singapore next month on the P. and O. liner, *The Osaka.*"

"To Singapore?"

The exclamation was almost a scream, and Lady Lettice Burne, sitting at the table, put down the cup she was holding with a hand that trembled.

"To . . . Singapore, Papa?" she repeated. "No . . . No . . . I cannot . . . do that!"

"Now, Letty," her father said soothingly, "we have discussed this before. You promised me that you were looking forward to marrying Maximus Kirby."

"Not in . . . Singapore, Papa! You said he would

1

come . . . here. Besides . . . that was a . . . long time
ago."

The words ended in a dismal whisper, and now Lady
Lettice's large blue eyes filled with tears.

"I do not want to . . . marry him, Papa! I do not
want to . . . marry . . . anyone!"

"That is ridiculous, Letty, as well you know!" the
Countess interposed.

Though her voice was quite sharp, her eyes were
apprehensive as they rested on her younger daughter.

"But, Letty, when Maximus Kirby came here," the
Earl said, speaking in a voice one might use to a small
child, "you found him very agreeable."

"He brought me the . . . little parrots," Letty said,
her voice still trembling, "and I thought that was . . .
kind of him. But I do not want to . . . marry him, and
I will not go . . . away from . . . home. I want to stay
with . . . you, Papa."

The Earl's eyes rested on his daughter's face with an
almost comical expression of dismay.

He could not bear tears and he always found it difficult to refuse anything Letty asked of him.

She was so lovely, and the Earl had an appreciation
of pretty women wherever he might find them.

There was no doubt that Lady Lettice Burne was
outstandingly beautiful. Her fair hair was like sunshine. Her pink-and-white complexion was flawless, her
blue eyes fringed with dark lashes, and her rosebud
mouth would have been the delight of any artist.

It might have been expected that Lady Lettice would
have been the toast, if not of London Society, at least
of all the eligible young gentlemen in the County.

But while they flocked to her side the first moment
she appeared, they most unaccountably soon turned
away in search of less beautiful, but more interesting
young women.

Therefore after her first Season in London, the Earl,
who was an intelligent man, faced the fact that his
younger daughter was not likely to make the brilliant
marriage he had envisaged for her.

There was always the hope, of course, that some elderly Peer would find her exquisite face a compensation for the almost infantile state of her intelligence, but at the moment he was not in evidence.

"It is not only that Letty has nothing to say but she does not appear even to listen!" the Earl said to his wife after one Ball, when, towards the end of the evening, he had noticed a singular lack of partners for the beautiful Lettice.

"I know, Hugo," the Countess had replied, "and I have explained to her over and over again that men expect a woman to concentrate on them; to listen to what they have to say; to laugh at their jokes."

"What the hell does she think about?" the Earl asked.

"Really, your language, Hugo!" the Countess expostulated.

"I apologise, my dear," the Earl said. "At the same time you must admit, it is exasperating! No-one could be lovelier than Letty, and I was looking forward to having a rich son-in-law."

The Countess sighed. There was no denying they had all been counting on it.

Alderburne Park was mortgaged up to the hilt. Their debts mounted year after year, and it seemed in fact that the only real asset they possessed was Lettice's unrivalled beauty.

Then when they had returned to the country and the Earl was most volubly resenting the expense that the London Season had cost him, Maximus Kirby had appeared.

At first the Earl had not thought of him as a prospective son-in-law.

Kirby had been introduced to him at White's Club by a fellow Peer who said in a voice which he thought to be "sotto voce," but which vibrated round the Morning-Room:

"I have just the fellow for you, Alderburne. Wants to buy horses to take back East. As rich as Croesus and prepared to pay exorbitant prices for anything that takes his fancy!"

This the Earl found was not quite true.

Maximus Kirby was by no means the "dupe" he had supposed from what his friend had told him.

He was certainly extremely wealthy, but he was shrewd enough to expect value for his money. Whilst he was prepared to pay over the odds for the Earl's best horses, he swept aside with a wave of his hand those which were not of first-class quality.

The Earl had invited him to Alderburne Park to see the horses.

It was the Countess who put the idea into her husband's head that Maximus Kirby was not only a very rich man but entirely presentable.

"I will say one thing," the Earl said to his wife, "Kirby may not be blue-blooded but he is certainly well-born. In fact he would pass anywhere for a gentleman."

"He is a gentleman!" the Countess said firmly, "and if he is slightly eccentric, or perhaps one might say a trifle flamboyant through living so long in the East, that does not make him in any way a less desirable party."

"Are you suggesting . . . ?" the Earl asked half-incredulously.

"I saw him looking at Letty last night after dinner," the Countess said. "I think, Hugo, that you will find that he will offer for her before he leaves."

"But Letty would have to live abroad!" the Earl exclaimed. "Kirby has huge estates, so I am told, in Malaysia."

"Since the Suez Canal was opened ten years ago," the Countess replied, "it does not now take nearly so long to reach the East. Why, Lord Avon was saying only last week that one can now get to India in twenty-five days!"

"He is certainly presentable," the Earl said slowly, and he was not speaking of Lord Avon.

"I found him delightful," the Countess offered.

There was no doubt that Mr. Kirby had a firm ally in Letty's mother.

What woman had ever been able to resist that strange, buccaneering, raffish charm which gives a man who has it an indefinable fascination.

Besides the fact that women were automatically drawn to him, Maximus Kirby was also a sportsman, which made him popular with his own sex.

He had, it was true, an audacity which made many jealous husbands and lovers grit their teeth, but he was also good-mannered, appreciative, and his vivid, magnetic personality seemed to bring to Alderburne Park a breath of fresh air that had been lacking before he came to stay.

He bought not only the Earl's best horses; he also made an offer which was eagerly accepted for several pictures, a Queen Anne lacquered cabinet and a number of books from the Library which the Earl had not even glanced at since he inherited.

Only Dorinda, when Mr. Kirby had left, noted the empty shelves with a feeling of dismay, because she knew they would never be filled again.

It was to Dorinda, sitting on the other side of the breakfast-table, that Letty appealed now with misty eyes and lips that trembled.

"You know, Dorinda . . . that I cannot . . . marry," she said in soft child-like tones. "Make Papa understand that I do not . . . like men. They . . . frighten me."

"Mr. Kirby is different," Dorinda answered. "Think how kind he was in giving you those pretty little parakeets, and I am sure that when you go to Singapore you can have a whole aviary of exotic birds. How exciting that would be!"

"I would like an aviary . . . here," Lettice said.

"It is too cold for them, they would die. Even the parakeets shiver however near the fire we put them."

Dorinda's voice was firm but at the same time beguiling.

Yet Lettice with her blue eyes fixed on her sister's face only looked a picture of beauty in distress.

She was one of the few people who looked directly at Dorinda. It was perhaps because she was lost in her own thoughts that she did not see her sister's face as others did.

It would have been noticeable to anyone watching the family at the breakfast-table that the Earl, even when he spoke to his elder daughter, did not look straight at her.

Dorinda by this time was used to people staring in another direction when they addressed her.

Nearly twenty-one, she had accepted the fact that she would never marry. At the same time it was hard to hear Lettice, who was so beautiful, affirming as she did so often that she was frightened of men.

Dorinda seldom had a chance of conversation with any man other than her father or the servants.

Ever since childhood she had suffered from a disfiguring skin complaint which covered her face, her arms and her legs with unsightly scaly patches.

It was easy to hide her wrists, which at times looked almost raw, and of course her legs. But there was nothing anyone could do about the horror of her upper lip or the great patches, red and peeling, which permanently disfigured her forehead and her chin.

At first the Doctors to whom the Countess took her declared it was only a symptom of adolescence.

"Many girls have bad complexions at that age," they said and prescribed a number of creams and lotions which did nothing to heal and usually increased the irritation.

When Dorinda was seventeen the Countess was frantic.

It was time to arrange for Dorinda's presentation at Court; for her to have a Season in London, for them to give a Ball for her at Alderburne Park.

Yet what was the use of wasting money on a girl from whom people winced away, if not in dusgust, certainly in pity.

There were also a number of those who suspected the complaint was infectious, an idea which the Doctors declared was ridiculous.

"But how can we tell people it is not catching?" Dorinda asked, "unless I wear a placard saying so?"

There had been nothing anyone could do, and in the end it was Dorinda who decided that she had no intention of forcing herself upon a Society which did not want her.

"Just forget about me, Mama," she said to her mother, "and save your money for Letty. She is going to be lovely, as we all know, and nothing you can do can make me look anything but horrible!"

It was true, although the Countess did not wish to admit it.

Pretty dresses and elaborate bonnets only seemed to accentuate Dorinda's deformity, and so in the end they all accepted the inevitable.

Dorinda stayed at home and seldom left Alderburne Park except to look after Letty who clung to her sister and could seldom be persuaded to go anywhere without her.

Dorinda's tact, or perhaps her shyness in not forcing herself upon people who did not want her, became a habit which in time everyone took for granted.

She often had to escort Letty to the very door of a party or a Ball-Room, because otherwise she would not go. Then unnoticed Dorinda would vanish.

She became expert at running Alderburne Park, without being seen when people came to stay.

Sometimes she used to tell herself with a wry smile that she was like one of the ghosts which were supposed to haunt the Grand-Staircase and the West Wing. But, unlike the ghosts, Dorinda was extremely useful.

"Oh, leave it to Dorinda!" the Earl would say. "She knows what I require."

"You will have to ask Lady Dorinda about the menu, Chef," the Countess would remark. "You know I can never remember the names of these new-fangled dishes."

"I want Dorinda. Where is Dorinda? I want her!" Letty would whine.

Only Dorinda could coax her into a good mood, get her downstairs in time for dinner or arrange her hair so skilfully that there was never any need to employ a professional hairdresser.

It was Dorinda who had tried in the past year to make Letty's marriage seem something exciting, an event to which she must look forward.

"Think how wonderful it will be to live always in sunshine!" she would say to Letty on a dull day. "Think what flowers there are in Singapore! I believe you can have a whole garden filled with orchids. And there are lovely birds, Letty, brilliant and colourful. You will love them!"

'I might have known,' Dorinda thought now, 'that Papa would break the news to Letty so tactlessly and upset her.'

"I am not . . . going away," Letty was saying. "I am going to stay . . . here with Dorinda and you . . . Papa. I love you! I am very . . . happy. I do not want to be . . . married!"

"But Letty, think what glorious clothes you can have," the Earl coaxed, "and fabulous jewellery! Maximus Kirby will be able to give you far finer diamonds than I have ever been able to buy for Mama, and of course pearls! There are marvellous pearls in the East and I am told one can buy them there more cheaply."

"I do not like . . . pearls," Letty pouted.

The Earl looked hopelessly across the table at his wife.

"I think, Hugo, we had better leave Dorinda to talk to Letty about the journey," the Countess said diplomatically.

"I have to send Kirby a cable," the Earl remarked. "He is expecting Letty to sail on the tenth of January."

"I am not going!" Letty declared, getting up suddenly from the table. "I am not going away! I am going to stay here! You do not love me . . . you do not want me . . . but I am not going to leave . . . leave whatever you . . . may say!"

She burst into tears as she spoke and ran from the room, looking so lovely and graceful as she did so that her father stared after her with a look of admiration rather than of anger in his eyes.

"You will have to persuade her, Dorinda," he said finally.

"Surely Mr. Kirby does not expect Letty to travel to Singapore alone?" the Countess questioned.

"Of course not," the Earl replied. "He says in his letter he is sure we will wish a companion to accompany her, and that he has arranged for Lady Anson, wife of the Lieutenant Governor of Panang, who will be travelling on the same ship, to chaperon Letty."

"A companion?" the Countess exclaimed. "Now who can we possibly find? A lady whom Letty will like and who is willing to go to Singapore!"

"There must be somebody," the Earl said with a note of irritation in his voice.

"Of course there must," the Countess retorted, "but I cannot imagine who. Is Mr. Kirby also paying the fare for a lady's-maid?"

Again the Earl consulted the letter.

"Yes, indeed, he says that he has sent a Chinese woman well experienced in her job on a ship that has already left. He has apparently made arrangements with the Shipping Line so that she will be on board *The Osaka* at Tilbury when Letty embarks."

"I must say he is very considerate," the Countess said in a mollified tone.

"Well, it would not have been convenient to send one of our own maids," the Earl said. "And anyway Letty will have to get used to Chinese servants."

"I believe they are excellent," the Countess said with a touch of envy in her voice. "Honest, hard-working and loyal to their employers."

"Then there is no problem about the lady's-maid," the Earl remarked. "But what about the companion?

Obviously Letty will have to have someone with her
who can keep her in a good mood."

"I will have to go with her, Papa," Dorinda said
quietly.

The Earl seemed startled.

"You, Dorinda? Surely that would be . . ."

He paused as if choosing his words.

". . . embarrassing," his daughter completed the
sentence. "Yes, of course it would be, Papa, if I went
as myself. But I shall not do that. I shall simply go as
Letty's companion and nobody will know that I am
really her sister."

There was a silence while her parents were digesting
the idea, until Dorinda said:

"As soon as Letty is safely married I will then return."

"Alone on a ship?" the Countess exclaimed.

"I will be quite safe, Mama," Dorinda said with a
touch of amusement in her voice.

"Yes, yes, of course," the Earl said in an embarrassed
manner. "At the same time it is hardly the behaviour
anyone would expect from a daughter of mine."

"No-one will know I am your daughter," Dorinda
said. "I will just call myself 'Miss Somebody-or-Other.'
Any name which sounds quiet and unobtrusive will do.
I can keep Letty happy. If I do not go, I doubt, when
she does arrive, if she will marry Mr. Kirby."

There was a silence as if all three people at the table
were remembering how awkward and difficult Letty
could be if it suited her.

Her fear of being married was the result of a very
unfortunate incident that had happened two years previously.

Because Letty was so beautiful and because the Earl
wished to show her off, he had taken her to a Hunt Ball
when she was not quite sixteen.

It was not an unprecedented act because quite a
number of the younger members of the Hunt who had
not yet made their débuts did attend the Hunt Ball with

their parents. In fact several girls of Lettice's age were to be present.

Wearing a new gown from London with a wreath of white roses in her hair, Lettice outshone every other woman in the room, whatever her age.

The Ball had been the usual frolic, and unfortunately the Earl enjoyed himself so much with his hunting and racing cronies that he could not be persuaded to leave when his wife suggested it.

In some way which the Countess could never quite account for, Letty had become separated from her, and a rather dissolute young sportsman who had imbibed too freely had kissed her.

In his defence it might be said that he found Letty's vacant stare and the fact that she did not protest at the first overtures he made to her a convincing proof that she was not unwilling.

He did not realise that she was completely unaware of his intention. In fact at first she did not even understand what he was saying. Then she was so paralysed with fear that she was unable to move or speak.

He kissed her passionately and had only released her when she had fallen at his feet in a dead faint.

The Countess had been sent for to receive a somewhat incoherent apology and had taken home a half-insensible, terrified Letty to turn her over to Dorinda's ministrations.

With any ordinary girl such an episode might easily have been forgotten or become a joke but on Letty it left an ineradicable scar. It made her wince away even from the quietest and most innocuous young man, lest he would assault her.

"You cannot be frightened of so-and-so," Dorinda would say. "He is the most unassuming man."

"I do not want to . . . dance with him," Letty would reply. "I do not like men to touch me."

"But Letty, dear, they are not going to hurt you."

"They . . . look at me! They say . . . things," Letty would protest.

"They are only telling you how beautiful you are,"

Dorinda explained. "You like being beautiful, Letty, you know you do!"

"I like you and Papa to think I am beautiful. But I do not want men to . . . look at me."

"It is ridiculous, Dorinda!" the Countess had said not once but a dozen times to her elder daughter. "She must have grown out of such childish ideas by now!"

"We will have to give her time, Mama," Dorinda remarked soothingly.

In her own mind she realised that Letty was not finding it any easier as she grew older to be in the company of gentlemen—in fact rather the opposite.

"Surely," the Earl asked now with a note of exasperation in his voice, "Letty is not really going to back out of marrying Kirby?"

"You heard what she said, Papa," Dorinda answered.

"Well, she cannot do it!" the Earl said firmly. "For once I am going to put my foot down. Girls marry whom they are told to marry, and there is no argument about it."

He paused for a moment and added:

"Why, the Duke was saying only last week he had no nonsense with his daughters, and after all he has seven of them! He has married them all off to wealthy noblemen, and I wager he did not have to put up with this sort of flapdoddle!"

"The trouble is, Hugo, you have spoiled Letty ever since she was a child," the Countess said accusingly.

"Dammit all! How was I to know she was going to behave in such an abnormal manner?" the Earl asked angrily.

He got up from the table pushing back his chair almost aggressively.

"God knows," he stormed, "it is bad enough not having a son to inherit! But to have two daughters— and both of them peculiar—is more than any man could endure!"

"Really, Hugo!" the Countess expostulated, "how can you speak so unkindly of poor Dorinda?"

The Earl's eyes glanced for a second towards his

elder daughter, but even before he could speak Dorinda said:

"It is all right, Papa, I quite understand. You owe Mr. Kirby money, do you not? So Letty must marry him!"

"Hugo!" the Countess cried. "Is this true?"

The Earl walked across to the fireplace where a log-fire was burning brightly in the grate.

"Well, as a matter of fact, my dear . . ." he began.

"How could you?" the Countess interposed. "To be in his debt before Letty has even got the ring on her finger! It is too humiliating!"

"Well, I was short at the time," the Earl replied, "and as he had taken six of my best horses, I had to have some money."

"What happened to the money that he paid you for the horses?" the Countess enquired.

"Need you ask?" the Earl replied bitterly. "The duns were at the gates, curse them, as you would have known if you ever listened to anything I told you. It was either a case of cutting down to bare bones and giving up the house or touching Kirby."

The Countess pressed her lips together.

Despite her undoubted good looks, she always looked cold and austere. Now she appeared almost formidable as she asked harshly:

"How much did you borrow in the confidence that as your son-in-law he would not ask you to return it?"

There was a pregnant silence before the Earl said:

"If you want to know the truth, ten thousand quid!"

The Countess gave an exclamation of horror. Then without another word she went from the room.

Dorinda looked at her father.

"I am sorry, Papa. I should not have said that."

"There was nothing else I could do, Dorinda," the Earl replied. "The debts had piled up and Kirby was only too glad to let me have the money in return for the promise that Letty would marry him."

Dorinda gave a little sigh.

"If she refuses now, Papa, you will have to give it back."

"But you know as well as I do that I cannot possibly do so. You have seen the accounts. They are no secret from you."

"Yes, I know, Papa, and I agree you could not possibly find ten thousand pounds unless you sold the house and what is left of the family pictures."

"I doubt if even that would bring in ten thousand pounds," the Earl remarked despondently.

"I am sure you are right," Dorinda sighed.

The Earl walked from the fireplace across to the window to stare out at the garden white with snow.

"I thought that once Lettice was married," he said, "it would be easy to suggest I buy horses for Kirby to ship to Singapore—or anything else that interested him. He is rich enough to be able to afford the little profit I should make on such transactions, and it would mean a great deal to me."

"I know, Papa," Dorinda said. "So somehow we have to persuade Letty to marry him. I did not want to say anything in front of Mama, but she has told me over and over again she would rather die than be touched by a man, whoever he might be."

"Good God!" the Earl ejaculated. "I ought to have murdered that swine who kissed her!"

"If we are honest with each other," Dorinda said quietly, "we both know that if it had not been him it would have been someone else. Letty is not like other girls."

"But she is beautiful, Dorinda. The most beautiful creature one could imagine. Surely she must have some normal feelings? Women want to be loved. They want to be married."

"Not all women."

"She will like it when she gets used to the idea," the Earl said as if trying to convince himself. "All you have to do, Dorinda, is to persuade her that Kirby will be kind and gentle with her, and tell Kirby he has to be."

He paused for a moment and then said:

"I imagined of course that he would come over here. I was going to speak to him myself of those matters."

"Why do you not go to Singapore with Letty, Papa?" Dorinda asked.

"For two very good reasons," the Earl replied. "One is that Kirby has not sent me the fare, and the second is that racing starts in another month and I have to be here for the Spring Handicaps, as you well know."

"Yes, of course," Dorinda agreed, "and it would be no use sending Mama. She had no patience with Letty and that does not help."

"I must admit Letty is enough to try the patience of a Saint," the Earl said. "Only you can do anything with her, Dorinda."

"So you agree to my going out to Singapore with her?"

"I have no alternative, although God knows what we shall do without you while you are gone."

Dorinda began to believe in the following weeks this was the truth.

There were so many things for her to see to before she left. Sometimes she went to bed feeling almost too tired to think.

There was not only Letty to keep as calm as possible but there were her clothes to buy, and the task of handing over all the jobs in the household which Dorinda had done as a matter of course.

These had to be allotted to members of the staff who were either resentful at being given the extra work or apprehensive about the responsibility.

It was Dorinda who planned everything down to the last detail.

"I shall call myself Miss Hyde," she told her father, "and as I am to be a companion, it would be best for me to look a little older than I actually am—not that anyone will look at me anyway!"

Her father did not contradict her and she continued:

"I have ordered myself some new gowns and you will have to pay for them. They are not very expensive and they are all in grey—a soft pigeon-breast grey, but nevertheless grey. I do not want to be noticed, and Letty's clothes must be all in the pretty gay colours which suit her so well."

"Get what you like, Dorinda," the Earl remarked. "As a matter of fact you need not feel you have to be too economical, as Kirby has sent me a cheque for expenses. He had already paid for the tickets so there was plenty to spare."

"Oh, Papa, and you were not going to say anything about it!" Dorinda said accusingly.

The Earl looked a little shame-faced.

"The fact is I did not want your mother to know," he confessed. "She disapproves of my borrowing money from anyone, and now she realises I am so deeply in debt to Kirby I did not dare confess to having accepted a further sum from him."

"It is much better not to worry Mama," Dorinda agreed and her father put his hand on her shoulder.

"You are a good girl, Dorinda, and far more sensible than any son could be. It is a pity . . ."

He left the sentence unfinished, and Dorinda knew there was for him a continual feeling of frustration that his marriage had produced only two daughters and not very satisfactory ones at that.

That night she looked at herself in the mirror in her bed-room, then glanced away from the terrible marks on her upper lip and forehead.

'If only I were pretty like Letty,' she thought. 'I would have married somebody who could help Papa, and he would have been so proud and thrilled if I could have become a Marchioness or perhaps a Duchess!'

Then she thought of Maximus Kirby and felt a little quiver go through her.

From a first-floor window she had watched him arrive when he came to stay.

He stepped out of the Phaeton in which her father had driven him down from London and she thought she had never seen a more arresting-looking man.

She had not at that moment been able to observe every detail of his face, and yet something in his broad shoulders, in the angle at which he wore his top-hat, the way he held his head, made her think that Maximus Kirby would be outstanding among other men wherever they might be.

She had run from the window to the top of the stairs to see him come into the Hall.

Crouching down, she had peeped through the bannisters as she had so often done as a child, and as he entered through the front door, she had seen him full-face and known that something strange had happened to her heart.

Never had she imagined that a man could look so fascinatingly interesting.

His features were by no means classical: the boldness of his eyes, the twist of his lips and the squareness of his chin combined to give him a face which she knew that she, and perhaps no other woman, could ever forget.

Maximus Kirby had stayed at Alderburne Park for two nights, and during that time he had never met Dorinda.

He had no idea she watched him.

There was a Minstrels' Gallery in the Banqueting-Hall, and through the heavy carving which had been intended to conceal the Minstrels in ancient days from those who dined, Dorinda had watched her father's guest.

She had seen him walk upstairs—she had seen him walk down. She had been at the windows as her father showed him the house from the outside and took him to the Stables.

She had been listening at the half-open door when he was introduced to Letty and when he gave her the gay, twittering little parakeets he had brought with him from Singapore.

Dorinda had heard his deep voice, and the tones of it seemed to vibrate within her. She had listened spellbound when her father talked about Mr. Kirby when he was not present and knew that even her mother's cold voice seemed to have a new warmth in it.

It was an understood thing that Dorinda never appeared when there were guests in the house.

On the second night of Maximus Kirby's visit, Dorinda had sat at her mirror for a long time wondering how she could disguise the marks on her face and for once go down to dinner.

Her father had invited a number of the neighboring nobility to dine. They had all accepted, eager to meet the man who Dorinda realised had made quite a stir in London.

"Everyone is talking about Mr. Kirby," Dorinda heard the wife of the Lord Lieutenant say. "I hear that the Queen has asked him to Windsor Castle. She wishes to hear personally of the wonders he has performed in Singapore."

"What are they?" the Earl had asked with interest.

"You must get my husband to tell you how Mr. Kirby has improved the Port and erected new buildings and done dozens of other things which I cannot now remember!" the Duchess had replied.

'I want to hear about it,' Dorinda had told herself.

Then as her reflection stared back at her, she had seen there were some new scaly incrustations on her eye-lids at the corners of her eyes.

This was due to the fact that she had gone hunting the previous week. It was the one amusement that she permitted herself outside the house.

Even so she did not go to the Grand Meets or hunt on the days when there was a big field, preferring the off-days when there were fewer people out.

As she was an exceptionally good rider, it was easy to keep ahead of the chattering other women on horseback and she would sometimes be the only follower left at the end of the day when everyone else had either been tailed off or had gone home.

The cold wind, the frost in the air and beating rain took its toll. Her eczema, for that was what the Doctors told her was the name of her skin complaint, was invariably worse after a hard day's hunting.

'It is worth it!' Dorinda would tell herself even while

she was kept awake at night by the irritation of it.

But now because she wanted so much to meet Maximus Kirby, she hated the scaly, fissured condition of her face more than she had ever hated it before.

How could she go downstairs and appear in the Drawing-Room looking as she looked now? It would be an unspeakable agony to know that Maximus Kirby would stare at her with distaste, if not disgust, and then, like everyone else, look away embarrassed by what he saw.

She watched him leave the house the following morning, and by that time the whole household knew that he had offered for Letty's hand and the Earl had agreed that in a year's time, when she was eighteen, they could be married.

"It has been a very happy visit," Dorinda heard Maximus Kirby say to her father in the Hall.

"We have greatly enjoyed having you, Kirby," the Earl replied. "I wish you could stay longer."

"I wish I could," Maximus Kirby replied, "but I am going to Windsor tomorrow and then the following day I start my journey back to Singapore."

"I am sure you will be glad to get back to the sunshine," the Earl remarked genially.

"It is actually back to work," Maximus Kirby had replied. "I came here principally to buy new machines, new equipment and find new contractors for the plans I am putting in hand for development of the town, the harbour, and reclamation of the jungle. It is all that in which Her Majesty is interested."

"I hear you have performed miracles," the Earl remarked, "and that they call you the 'Uncrowned King of Singapore'!"

Maximus Kirby threw up his hands in mock dismay.

"Her Majesty would be horrified at the idea! No, I am but an humble servant of Britain, and I am in fact only carrying on the plan originated by Sir Thomas Raffles. It is to him that this country owes the possession of Singapore."

"He was a great man," the Earl remarked.

"Very great in the part of the world I come from," Maximus Kirby agreed. "I hope one day you will visit me and see for yourself what he himself largely created."

"I shall hope to do that," the Earl answered.

There was silence for a moment and then Maximus Kirby said:

"I will write to you about the arrangements for the marriage. I wish first to complete the house I am building. I am sure that Lady Lettice will like it."

"I am sure she will," the Earl agreed hastily.

"Then good-bye and thank you again," Maximus Kirby said.

The two men shook hands and Mr. Kirby walked down the steps to where the Phaeton was waiting for him.

Dorinda watched him leave the Hall, and then she ran swiftly up to a bed-room which overlooked the front of the house.

He had already climbed into the high seat of the Phaeton and had apparently told the groom that he would drive, for the reins were in his hands.

He held them and his whip at exactly the angle which was considered correct by all the experts who tooled their own horses.

It was cold and he was wearing a caped driving-coat, and his hat was set at an angle at the side of his dark hair. He looked majestic—a splendid and commanding figure of a man, one who no doubt expected to arouse admiration wherever he went.

And yet there was something more, Dorinda told herself.

There was a power about him, a compelling vitality, something she had sensed ever since he had been in the house. Now, she thought despairingly, he was going away and she would never see him again.

Yet he was unforgettable.

It was as if they had been visited by an inhabitant from another world, which indeed, Dorinda told herself, was the truth.

He was not a part of England. He was a visitor from the other side of the universe and perhaps in reality they had little in common.

Below her, the Earl stood on the steps to wave his guest good-bye. Maximus Kirby raised his top-hat.

Dorinda saw he was smiling.

She had the feeling it was the smile of a man who had got exactly what he wanted.

There was a triumphant twist to his lips and a glint in his eyes which told her he was well satisfied.

'I wonder what has pleased him so much?' she asked herself and knew the answer.

Maximus Kirby had come to Alderburne Park to find himself a wife, and that was exactly what he had achieved!

Chapter Two

Dorinda started to unpack in her Cabin aboard *The Osaka*.

It was one of the latest P. & O. Ships which served the Far East, and she was pleasantly surprised at the comfort and luxury of the State-Rooms she and Letty had been allotted.

There were two large cabins to sleep in and a State-Room in which there were several huge baskets of expensive flowers ordered for Letty with the compliments of Maximus Kirby.

They had been received on board with an impressive formality, almost as if, Dorinda thought to herself, they were Royalty.

When the Chinese lady's-maid appeared, bowing low, it was impossible not to realise how extremely fortunate and comfortable they were.

But Letty had been in a querulous, miserable state for weeks.

She had insisted over and over again that she did not wish to go to Singapore, did not want to be married and that all she desired was to stay at home with her parents.

The Earl was so bored with it that he used to leave the house early in the morning and returned only at night, often after dinner.

The Countess shut herself in her own Sitting-Room and declared she had such a headache she could cope

22

with no more of Letty's complaints. As usual, everything was left to Dorinda.

Letty had taken no interest in the pretty clothes which had been bought for her trousseau. In fact half the time she refused even to try on the gowns and Dorinda had to fit them for her.

Both the girls were of a similar build, although usually Dorinda was slightly slimmer than her sister. But through fretting, complaining and refusing to eat, Letty had lost weight.

The dress-makers fitted the clothes on Dorinda and kept her standing for hours while she thought anxiously about all the other important things she had to do.

The Earl and Countess took their daughters to London and stayed for ten days so that Letty could be dressed in the very latest and most up-to-date fashion.

The clothes were in fact so entrancing and so obviously expensive that the Countess asked suspiciously how they were to be paid for, but neither the Earl nor Dorinda enlightened her.

Letty was more than usually difficult in London, weeping if her father tried to discuss her wedding with her and not answering when their friends offered her their good wishes.

"If Kirby sees Letty in this state," the Earl said privately to Dorinda, "he will call the whole thing off. Let us hope that he is so bemused by her beauty he does not attempt to talk to her until the ring is on her finger."

Dorinda could not but wonder if in fact they were cheating the "Uncrowned King of Singapore." Then she told herself that if they were it was entirely his own fault!

She was certain there was some special reason why he required a wife, and she was determined to discover the answer later.

Thinking of Maximus Kirby's arresting face, she was sure there must be thousands of women all over the world who would jump at the opportunity of becoming his bride and would love him whole-heartedly.

Why then had he come to England and chosen Letty, knowing so little about her?

Dorinda thought to herself that her father's rank must have something to do with it.

After all they might be comparatively poor, but Alderburne was a name that went far back into the history of England and the family had been both powerful and respected all down the ages.

There had been Alderburnes at the Court of Elizabeth who had proved themselves great statesmen. There had been Alderburnes who had supported the Restoration of the Monarchy in the reign of Charles II, and Alderburnes in the seats of power in the reign of Queen Anne.

It was perhaps because they had been so honest and so selfless in serving their country rather than themselves, that the wealth they handled for their Monarchs never found its way into their own pockets.

But one thing was certain, Dorinda thought, her father had procured himself a rich son-in-law.

In London Dorinda went out of her way to discover more about Maximus Kirby.

It was not difficult to get her father to ask questions of the Colonial Secretary and even the Prime Minister about the politics and development of Singapore.

"I must try to get Letty interested in her future husband's affairs before she sees him again, Papa," was an excuse which made the Earl produce all the information she required.

She learnt among other things that it was due to Maximus Kirby that the Port at Singapore was the success that had been envisaged at the beginning of the century by a brilliant and adventurous young Englishman.

Sir Thomas Stamford Raffles, who was born on a merchant ship of which his father was the Captain, had become, at the age of fourteen, a clerk in the offices of the East India Company.

When he was twenty-four he was sent to Penang, where he immediately made his mark, and when the

English occupied Java, he became Lieutenant Governor. At his departure the people declared they had lost the greatest friend they had ever possessed.

In 1818 he envisaged the idea of breaking the Dutch Monopoly in the Straits Settlements by making Singapore a great free port. Despite strenuous opposition and many difficulties he accomplished this six years later.

"I understand Kirby has practically exterminated the pirates!" the Earl told her. "At one time they were doing so much damage in the Malay Peninsula that trade was almost at a stand-still, even though the Government did send war-ships to deal with them."

"War-ships, Papa?" Dorinda asked fascinated.

"Several cruisers were in action in the 1830's and during the next twenty years there was a special anti-piracy flotilla," the Earl replied. "But what is amusing is that in 1837 a steamer, *The Diana* was sent to Singapore and became the first Colonial steamer to go into battle against pirates."

"Tell me about it," Dorinda begged.

"The First Lord of the Admiralty was very voluble on the matter," the Earl replied. "Apparently it made Naval history."

"What happened with *The Diana*?" Dorinda asked.

"The First Lord told me she was the first steamer to be built in India and had a tonnage of a hundred sixty and a speed of five knots. Her crew consisted of three Europeans and thirty Malays."

"Go on, Papa," Dorinda prompted.

"In company with *H.M.S. Wolf*, which was a sailing craft, she started off on the first adventure. They found six large prahus, which is what the Chinese pirates call their ships, attacking a junk."

Dorinda was listening intently and the Earl continued:

"The pirates, seeing the smoke from 'Diana's' funnels took her to be a sailing ship on fire and scenting easy prey, they transferred their attack from the junk to the steam-ship."

The Earl laughed.

"To their horror the vessel came right up against the wind and fired into the prahus as she passed, turned and repeated the process."

"There could not have been much left of the pirate-ships after that," Dorinda remarked.

"There was not!" the Earl agreed.

"And this action eliminated the pirates?" Dorinda suggested.

"Not immediately," the Earl replied, "but it showed the authorities that something could be done to alleviate what had become an intolerable nuisance, with a number of important firms threatening to leave Singapore altogether."

"That must have happened years before Mr. Kirby became influential in Singapore," Dorinda said.

"He would have heard the story told and retold when he was a child," the Earl answered. "And when he began to have some authority he put his own ideas into action."

"What were they?"

"Kirby found that while the pirates had ceased to molest ships on the open sea for fear of reprisals, they continued to attack any vessel which was at anchor in a small harbour or sailing along an unfrequented part of the coast."

The Earl paused, as if recalling what he had been told.

"Apparently," he went on, "their invariable custom was to creep aboard very quietly, usually at night, and murder the crew and the passengers brutally before they could call for help."

"What did Mr. Kirby do about it?" Dorinda asked.

"He produced his own fleet of small, fast patrol boats all heavily armed, but much more easily maneuverable than war-ships. The First Lord says that in consequence piracy has almost ceased in the Malacca Straits."

Dorinda stored up every tiny detail and conscientiously attempted to interest Letty in what she learnt, but it was hopeless.

She had only to mention Maximus Kirby's name for her sister to start crying that she did not wish to be married.

In fact she became so distraught that finally Dorinda said to her father:

"What am I to do, Papa, if when we reach Singapore, Letty refuses to go through with the marriage ceremony?"

"She has to marry Kirby!" the Earl asserted, striking his desk at which he was sitting, with his clenched fist. "Good God, Dorinda, surely you can persuade a girl of that age to see the advantages of marrying such a man?"

Dorinda, without answering, only looked at her father, and after a moment he said in a different tone of voice:

"I know it is difficult. Perhaps I have set you an impossible task. But if she does refuse, we are all in the soup and make no mistake about it. I shall not only have to find the ten thousand pounds that Kirby loaned me, but I suppose I am also honour-bound to return his last cheque."

"Is it all spent, Papa?" Dorinda asked.

"Every penny!' her father replied.

When Dorinda heard that three more horses had been added to the Alderburne racing stables, she knew how!

Nevertheless her father had been generous over Letty's trousseau, and when the gowns were delivered everyone in the household, with the exception of the future bride, inspected them with delight and admiration.

"You will look beautiful in them," Dorinda told her sister.

"I want to look beautiful for Papa," Letty answered.

"If you love Papa, you will behave as he wishes you to behave," Dorinda said.

There was no doubt that Letty was fond of her father, and this was the only trump-card Dorinda had by which she could persuade Letty to embark on the journey to Singapore.

The night before they were actually to leave Alderburne Park, Letty had hysterics and tried to lock herself in her bed-room.

Dorinda both prevented her doing so by painting a dismal picture of the Earl having to sell his home, his horses and live in penury and succeeded in cajoling Letty into starting out the next morning.

"You cannot be so cruel to Papa whom you profess to love," Dorinda said sharply.

"I do love Papa . . . I do . . . I do," Letty averred.

"Then show your love by helping him," Dorinda said firmly. "If you fail him now, Letty, he may never want to see you again. How could he bear that one who is his own flesh and blood should behave so abominably?"

Letty appeared to be listening and Dorinda added:

"To back out of your engagement now would make Papa appear not only dishonourable, but even dishonest."

It was only after a tearful and heartbreaking farewell at Tilbury, which left her father and mother shaken and white-faced, that Letty consented to board *The Osaka*.

"It would be much better if you do not stay with her until the last moment," Dorinda said to her father. "Say good-bye and go away. She is certain to be frantic when she finds the ship is actually about to leave and, if she sees you are still there, she might try to get ashore."

As usual Dorinda was right.

When Letty heard the final call for non-sailing persons to leave the ship together with the bells ringing and the horn blowing and knew they were about to sail, she threw herself into a frenzy.

"I will not go . . . I will not! I want to go home! I want to be with . . . Papa!" she screamed.

"It is too late!" Dorinda said. "He is on his way back to London and so pleased and happy, Letty, that you are behaving so well."

Eventually Dorinda soothed her sister down and because she was so exhausted by her emotions, Letty fell asleep almost before the ship had begun to move down-river.

Closing the curtains over the port-hole, Dorinda went into her own Cabin.

The Chinese lady's-maid had unpacked for Letty as soon as they came aboard and offered to do the same for Dorinda. But the few possessions she had with her she preferred to arrange herself.

The new dresses, all soft grey with white collars and cuffs, looked very suitable for her position as Letty's companion and made her appear the shadowy figure she wished to be.

But in her trunks what interested her far more than her new gowns were a number of books.

Some she had bought in London, some she had newly discovered in the Library at Alderburne Park.

In London she had taken time off from pandering to Letty to visit not only a book shop in St. James's Street but also the British Museum.

Dorinda must have been twelve when she first realised that she was intelligent. It had been brought home to her very forcibly when she heard her Governess say to her father:

"The trouble is, My Lord, there is little more I can teach Lady Dorinda. She is so clever that she picks up the subject and absorbs it almost before I have time to explain it to her. It is a great tragedy she was not a boy."

Dorinda felt it was tactless of the Governess to remind her father of such an obvious fact, but the Earl had replied:

"I suppose, Miss Greenway, that what you are trying to tell me is that Dorinda should have additional tutors?"

"I think it would be a distressing waste if, with her ability, she has to rely for her education on the little I can teach her," Miss Greenway answered. "When I was engaged I explained to Her Ladyship that my capabilities are limited."

The Earl did not answer and Miss Greenway continued:

"I should be very sorry to leave Alderburne Park, My Lord, but I should not feel I was doing my duty unless I pointed out the truth, that Dorinda requires more experienced teaching than I am able to give her."

"No man wants a clever wife," the Earl had said with a note of irritation in his voice. "I am perfectly content with the manner in which you are teaching my daughters, Miss Greenway, and I have no intention of wasting either their time or my money on an education which will only make them restless and dissatisfied."

He paused before he said positively:

"All a woman needs to know is how to be a good wife and a good mother. Any other knowledge she can learn from her husband when she has one."

The Earl had left the School-Room when Dorinda entered through another door, and looking at Miss Greenway she saw something suspiciously like tears in her eyes.

"I have done my best for you, Dorinda," she said, "and failed. Now you will have to educate yourself."

It was Miss Greenway who had shown Dorinda that books could not only open the mind to new horizons, but also that they could be a solace and a comfort.

When Dorinda finally realised that nothing could be done about her skin complaint, it was through books that she learnt to escape into a world where such things were of no account, and not to brood over her own misfortunes.

One of the Harley Street Specialists to whom the Countess took her said:

"I have always found that people subject to eczema were extremely intelligent. I believe Julius Caesar was a life-long sufferer."

"Julius Caesar was a man," Dorinda answered quietly.

The Specialist said no more, but she remembered his words and found them a small consolation.

She taught herself by making a special study of any subject of which she realised she was ignorant.

First of all, because it gave her father pleasure, she learnt everything she could about racing; the breeding of horses; the training of them and the pedigrees of those who won important races.

She was the only person in the house to whom her father confided his hopes and ambitions on the race-course and to whom he came for consolation when his horses lost.

The Minstrel Gallery proved a stepping-stone to so many things Dorinda would not otherwise have known existed.

Usually the conversation at dinner was about sport but once her father entertained an eminent American Senator, which made her read the whole history of the United States.

On several occasions diplomats from Europe visited Alderburne Park and Dorinda made herself a walking encyclopaedia on the customs of the respective countries and the genealogy of their reigning Monarchs.

There were also subjects nearer home. She found birds fascinating but discovered that when she had learnt all about them making their nests, breeding and their migrations, it was impossible not to hate the idea of their being slaughtered for sport.

Dorinda regularly studied the current political situation. She was the only person in Alderburne Park who read *The Times* from cover to cover and found items of interest in the papers and magazines which her father bought only for their reports on horse-racing.

Now from her round-topped leather trunks she took out one by one the books she had accumulated for the voyage.

They were nearly all concerned with Chinese culture.

There was a book on jade, another on Chinese pottery, and several on Chinese painting.

She had found these with great difficulty, and when the assistant at the bookshop produced them she had been horrified at the amount they had cost.

However by having two fewer gowns than she had thought at first were necessary, she had managed to pay for them. She had also been fortunate to find two books in the Library at Alderburne Park which were concerned with the early history of the Malay Peninsula.

Dorinda touched the books with gentle fingers. Even to look at them gave her a feeling of delight.

There was so much there for her to learn. So much she wanted to know and understand.

She had visited the Chinese rooms of the British Museum, looked at the long, scroll-like pictures, and had known in a strange way that they meant something personal to her. It was something that she could not yet put into words even to herself, but she had the feeling that she had some indefinable link with them.

They were trying to tell her something. Something that perhaps lay half-forgotten in her memory, or else was part of a secret knowledge waiting to reveal itself.

It was with an effort that she forced herself to unpack the rest of her belongings. The mere fact that the books were lying on the table was an almost irresistible temptation. She wanted to open one—to let herself absorb all they could tell her.

Even the excitement of being on board ship paled beside the idea that the books had something to impart which it was important for her to know.

Then having tidied her Cabin, Dorinda put on the warm cape she had brought for travelling and went up on deck. They were moving out towards the open sea, but there was still land in view.

It was a grey, cold afternoon with the promise of either snow or rain in the sky. Dorinda looked to where the waves were already splashing over the bows and she drew in a deep breath.

She was starting off on a great adventure. She was going overseas. She was going to see Singapore.

'And who else?' she could not repress the thought.

She knew the answer even though like a horse that was frightened, she tried to shy away from it.

But the truth pressed itself upon her so that she could not avoid facing it.

She wanted to see Maximus Kirby again. She wanted to meet him as she had never wanted anything before in her whole life!

The sea became exceedingly rough as soon as they reached the English Channel. The weather grew worse and the sea more and more tempestuous as they turned South to run down the Coast of France.

Letty was immediately extremely sea-sick and very frightened.

"I am sure the ship is . . . going to . . . sink! We shall all go to the . . . bottom of the . . . ocean," she wailed.

For three days and nights Dorinda hardly left her side and then the Doctor intervened.

"You can't go on like this, Miss Hyde," he said to Dorinda. "I am going to call in someone to help you nurse Lady Lettice, otherwise I shall have not one but two invalids on my hands."

"I am quite all right, Dr. Johnson," Dorinda replied.

"How much sleep did you get last night?" he enquired.

As Dorinda did not answer he said:

"I do not intend to argue with you, Miss Hyde. I've already spoken to Sister Teresa and she's willing to come and give a hand. We know her well on this Line. She is a marvellous woman and greatly respected in the part of the world to which you are going."

"Is she a nurse?" Dorinda asked.

"She is a Missionary," Dr. Johnson replied. "I do not know if she had much success at converting the natives to Christianity, but she certainly improves their health. Where nursing is concerned she is first-class and when necessary as good as any Doctor."

Dorinda did not doubt his word when she met Sister Teresa. A woman of over forty, she had a quiet, competent assurance which inspired confidence wherever she went.

In her black habit and white wimple she would have seemed awe-inspiring, if it had not been for her infectious smile and bright, twinkling eyes.

"The Doctor tells me you have been having a difficult time with Lady Lettice," she said to Dorinda. "Well, you must allow me to take some of the nursing off your hands. It is what I am used to."

"It is very kind of you," Dorinda answered. "At the same time my friend is sometimes averse to meeting new people."

"She will soon get used to me," Sister Teresa answered quietly.

To her surprise Dorinda found she was right!

Letty seemed to take to the Sister almost at once, and it was an indescribable relief to Dorinda to see her doing what Sister Teresa suggested, and prepared to submit without any protest to her ministrations.

It was certainly a joy, apart from being able to have some sleep to have a little time on her hands for reading.

It was almost impossible however, to get much exercise with the ship still pitching and tossing.

Although Dorinda forced herself to go on deck at least twice a day, she was completely content to curl up on a sofa in the private State-Room and forget everything but the book she held in her hands.

By the time they were through the Bay of Biscay and were moving into the comparatively quiet waters of the Mediterranean, it was obvious that Letty was completely content to be in the company of Sister Teresa.

She even seemed to like being read to, which was something Dorinda had never been able to achieve.

"I am extremely grateful to you, Doctor Johnson," Dorinda said to the jovial, good-humoured man, whom she had learnt by now was quite a personality on the P. & O. Liners.

"I have never known Sister Teresa fail to get her own way when it comes to coaxing a patient back to life or a fretful child into eating a sensible meal." Dr. Johnson replied. "That reminds me, Miss Hyde. There is no excuse now for you not to come down to meals in the Dining-Salon."

Dorinda looked uncomfortable.

"I prefer to have my meals alone, Doctor," she said and wondered why he had not the tact to realise that she did not wish to be seen.

"Well you certainly have a comfortable place to eat in," the Doctor remarked.

That evening Sister Teresa asked Dorinda to go to the Doctor's Surgery for some medicine he had prepared for Letty.

"It is a potion Lady Lettice finds settles her stomach," she told Dorinda, "and I informed the Doctor this morning that we were almost at the end of the bottle."

"I will fetch it," Dorinda answered.

She went below to the Surgery where the Doctor normally saw his patients, but there was no-one there.

A steward seeing Dorinda at the door told her that the Doctor was most likely to be in the Purser's office.

Dorinda went back onto the Upper Deck.

She knocked at the door of the Purser's private office and when it opened explained her errand.

Dr. Johnson was sitting in an arm-chair, a drink in his hand.

"Come in, Miss Hyde," he said jovially as he rose. "You have not yet had a chance to meet our Purser, but he is longing to make your acquaintance."

Dorinda looked at the Purser, a weather-beaten man of about fifty, in surprise.

"He is curious about your charge." Dr. Johnson smiled. "As you can imagine, the whole ship is talking about her."

"About Lady Lettice?" Dorinda asked.

"Who else?" the Doctor enquired. "The future bride of Maximus Kirby! He is of considerable importance in Singapore, as you must be well aware."

"I think I ought to be getting back to the cabin," Dorinda said uncomfortably, "if you would let me have the medicine you promised Sister Teresa."

"Now come along, Miss Hyde," Dr. Johnson said.

"You're not going to run away like that! As your Medical Practitioner I'm going to prescribe for you too. What you need is a glass of madeira and a confidential chat. You've been very unsociable ever since the start of this voyage."

Dorinda tried to protest but it was hopeless.

She could not withstand the friendliness of Dr. Johnson or refuse the glass of madeira which the Purser put in her hand.

It also struck her that here were two men who could tell her about Maximus Kirby, and she was to find that they had a great deal to say on that particular subject.

"Have you met the Mighty Max?" Dr. Johnson asked her.

"No, I have never met him," Dorinda answered truthfully. "Is that what you call him?"

"Most people in Singapore say *Al*mighty," the Purser laughed, "and it is a very apt description. He rules the place with an iron hand in a velvet glove and there is not a Chinaman who would not lie down and lick his boots, if he asked him to do so."

"Why do they admire him so much?" Dorinda enquired.

"First, because he brought them prosperity," the Doctor answered, "and secondly because he is the type of man they want to idolise."

"What is he like?" Dorinda asked.

The two men looked at each other and laughed.

"Go on, describe him," the Doctor said to the Purser.

"I can't," the Purser confessed. "I suppose 'fantastic' would be an apt description."

"Try 'fabulous'—'superb'—'over-whelming'—'autocratic'—'over-powering'! You name it—I'll agree to it," the Doctor laughed.

"I'm just wondering," the Purser said, "if Lady Lettice realises what she's letting herself in for? There's not a woman who will not be ready to scratch her eyes out for having snatched Max from under their very noses!"

Dorinda looked from one man to the other apprehensively.

She realised that because they thought she was just Lady Lettice's companion they were talking frankly in front of her.

What was more she had always found that because of her disfigurement few people treated her as an ordinary young woman.

She had received so many confidences, learnt so many secrets from all sorts and conditions of ordinary people, simply because in some strange way she seemed to be set apart from the usual man or woman with whom she came in contact.

Because she did not look normal, she did not seem normal, and so people were prepared to tell her things they would not have spoken of otherwise.

All the villagers in Alderburne had taken her into their confidence at some time or another, every servant working in the house or outside, looked on her as their friend.

"What is the bride like?" the Purser asked.

"Beautiful!" the Doctor replied. "I've never seen such a lovely girl! You needn't worry about the ladies in Singapore. She'll knock them all into a cocked-hat."

Dorinda smiled.

"I am very glad to hear you say that, Doctor."

"She'll need to be more than pretty to hold Max," the Purser remarked.

"What do you mean?" Dorinda asked.

"Well, Doctor Johnson and I have known a large number of Max's lady friends over the years," the Purser said, taking a sip of the whisky he was drinking from a long glass.

"That's true," the Doctor agreed. "Do you remember Perfect Pearl? Heavens, the money Max spent on that woman!"

"I bet she was worth it!" the Purser said. "Divine creature. Her name became her."

"Who was she?" Dorinda asked, trying to keep the note of surprise out of her voice.

"Chinese!" the Doctor explained. "Max found her in

Hong Kong. You have never seen anything so exotic or so exquisite."

"Max certainly saw she lived up to her name," the Purser remarked. "He gave her pearls the size of pigeons' eggs—ropes of them! I used to wonder sometimes how she managed to carry them on that tiny, swan-like neck of hers."

"It was diamonds for Goldie," the Doctor said.

"Goldie!" the Purser wagged his finger and laughed. "Will you ever forget those parties? God, but they were fun! Do you remember the one that went on for three days? When I finally got back on the ship I thought my head was going to split open!"

"Who was Goldie?" Dorinda asked in a very small voice.

"Australian," the Doctor answered. "Lovely girl. Hair like gold. Skin just touched by the sun and a laugh which seemed to ring out like a peal of bells."

"What happened to Perfect Pearl and Goldie?" Dorinda enquired.

"Max got tired of them," the Purser replied. "He tires easily. He's an adventurer, always seeking something new, always finding new lands to conquer."

"He certainly does not encounter much opposition," the Doctor chuckled.

The Purser glanced at Dorinda and then away again.

"What we are trying to find out, Miss Hyde, is whether your young lady is going to make Max a good wife and persuade him to settle down."

"I believe that's what he wants to do," the Doctor said.

"What—Max settle down?" the Purser laughed. "I'll believe that when I see it!"

"I've an idea he is modelling himself on his hero, Sir Thomas Raffles. If you remember, Raffles had a very remarkable wife who supported, encouraged and inspired him."

"You may be right," the Purser said seriously. "It'd be just like Max to go off on a new tack; to decide that marriage is for him and bring home a wife who'll eclipse all the other women he has ever known."

"Lady Lettice will certainy shine as one of the greatest beauties Singapore has ever seen," the Doctor said reflectively.

As he spoke Dorinda wondered if he realised just how childish Letty was, and his next words made her think that he had already summed her up.

"There's a great deal that the right sort of wife could do for Max," he said slowly, "but she'd have to be the right sort."

"Which by all accounts is exactly what we have aboard!" the Purser said enthusiastically. "Come along, Miss Hyde, we must drink to that and then I'll refill your glass."

"No, no, I could not drink any more. Thank you very much, Doctor, but if you will excuse me, I must be getting back to my Cabin."

Dorinda looked at the Doctor meaningfully, as if to make him realise that she really meant to leave, and he hoisted himself out of his comfortable armchair.

"I will bring the medicine to your State-Room, Miss Hyde," he said.

"Thank you, Doctor," Dorinda replied and turning to the Purser she added, "And thank you very much for your hospitality."

"Come and see me any time you feel lonely," the Purser said. "We shall be having a party as soon as the sea is calm enough."

"It is very kind of you," Dorinda answered, "but I never go to parties."

The Purser did not try to persuade her, and she realised that he understood her reasons for refusing such sociable occasions.

She went back to her Cabin and thought over what she had heard. She now faced the fact that not only was Letty's marriage likely to be a disaster, but her father was—in what would have been his own words—"selling Maximus Kirby a pup."

Kirby could have no idea that Letty was so brainless

and immature. He had seen her at Alderburne Park, but only in the company of her parents. He had doubtless thought, as had other men before him, that her silence was due to shyness.

Dorinda knew that her father had shown off Letty in her very best light. Also Letty had been genuinely delighted with the little parakeets and that would have left an impression of someone sweet and amenable, which were doubtless the qualities Mr. Kirby required of his wife.

What would he feel, Dorinda asked herself, when he learnt how querulous and difficult Letty could be; how incredibly stupid she was and how impossible it was for her to discuss even the most fundamental and common-place subjects of every-day life?

Would her beauty be enough, Dorinda asked herself, when he needed her to play hostess to the many notabilities who called on him in Singapore?

Would the way in which she would moon away a whole day playing with a kitten or watching her birds be anything but a bore when he wanted to tell her about his plans and ambitions?

'I must make her understand what she has to do,' Dorinda told herself desperately.

She wondered if anyone had ever had such a Herculean task to accomplish in so short a time.

She went into Letty's Cabin to find Sister Teresa sitting by her bed and reading aloud. She stopped as Dorinda entered.

"Did you get the medicine, Miss Hyde?" she asked.

"The Doctor is bringing it along in a few moments," Dorinda answered.

"You are interrupting, Dorinda," Letty protested. "Go on, Sister Teresa. I want to hear the end of the story."

There was a querulous note in Letty's voice which Dorinda knew meant tears and a small tantrum if she did not get her own way.

She smiled apologetically.

"Please continue the story," she said to Sister Teresa. "I will wait in the State-Room."

A few minutes later she heard a knock at the door and the Doctor entered.

"How is our patient?" he asked.

"Engrossed in a book that Sister Teresa is reading to her," Dorinda answered. "Unless you think it important, it would be better not to disturb her. I have never known Letty become so friendly with anyone so quickly, as she has with the Sister."

"I told you Sister Teresa has a magic touch," the Doctor smiled. "We will soon have Lady Lettice on her feet again."

"I am very grateful to you," Dorinda said.

"You have been behaving like a worried hen over that young woman," he said. "Have you known her a long time?"

"Oh, yes," Dorinda answered, "the whole of her life."

"That accounts for your consideration," he said. "Well, she is lucky to have you."

"And very lucky to have Sister Teresa!"

"That goes without saying," the Doctor smiled. "It was fortunate she was on this particular ship. As a matter of fact I do not mind telling you now that the Captain, and the Purser were in a panic in case Lady Lettice should become ill and bring the wrath of Almighty Max down upon their heads!"

Dorinda laughed.

"Is he really as important as all that?"

"That and a great deal more."

The Doctor hesitated a moment then he said in a somewhat apologetic voice:

"I hope you were not shocked by what we said just now. I thought afterwards it was not a conversation that should have taken place in front of a lady."

"You need not worry about anything you say in front of me," Dorinda said.

"I think what we were really trying to convey to you is that Maximus Kirby is a very exceptional person.

Therefore everyone will expect the wife he has chosen to be exceptional, too."

Dorinda was silent for a moment and then she said:

"Are you suggesting, Doctor, that you think Lady Lettice, from what you have seen of her, is not the right wife for him?"

The Doctor did not answer at once. Then he said slowly:

"I am not making any statements or offering any criticisms, Miss Hyde. Lady Lettice is one of the most beautiful girls I have ever seen in my life—perhaps the most beautiful—but I cannot help asking myself what else she has to offer Max the Mighty!"

Chapter Three

"Lady Anson's compliments, and as Her Ladyship is not well enough to call on Lady Lettice Burne, she would be very grateful if Her Ladyship would graciously visit her State-Room."

The Steward repeated the message almost breathlessly as if he was afraid to forget one word of it.

Dorinda, who had put down her book to listen to him, smiled.

"Will you thank Lady Anson for her kind invitation and tell her that unfortunately Lady Lettice Burne is not well enough herself at the moment to leave her Cabin or receive visitors?"

"Very good, Miss."

The Steward went from the Cabin and Dorinda picked up her book again.

This exchange of messages had taken place almost every day since the sea had grown calmer. Dorinda realised that Lady Anson was doing her best to be an efficient Chaperon despite the fact that she herself had been incapacitated ever since they had sailed.

There was no question of Letty seeing anyone at the moment except Sister Teresa.

She had not only been physically ill owing to the roughness of the sea, but this coming on top of her very low spirits at leaving home, the combination of what was both mental and physical anguish, had left her in a state of collapse.

"Don't try to make her do anything," Dr. Johnson

told Dorinda. "Let her relax. She'll feel better when we reach the sunshine."

He spoke as if the sun was a panacea for all ills but Dorinda was sceptical whether the climate would in any way affect Letty's attitude.

However she was sincerely grateful to Sister Teresa for nursing Letty so effectively. She had even ensured that Dorinda was seldom awakened more than once or twice during the night.

Dorinda herself was happy as long as she could read.

She took her exercise now that they were in calmer waters early in the morning when there were few people on deck. Except of course the ardent health-fiends who were determined to walk a hundred times around the deck at least twice a day.

Most of the people on board, Dorinda noticed, were rather dull.

There were Rubber Planters and their wives going out to Malaya for the first time, clerks leaving England to take up posts in the East India Company, and a number of businessmen who spent most hours of the day and night seated at the Bar in the Smoking-Saloon.

Dorinda did not find it lonely having so few people to talk to. She liked Sister Teresa and found her very interesting.

The Sister came into the State-Room now, closing the door of Letty's Cabin behind her.

"Is she asleep?" Dorinda asked.

The Sister nodded.

"Can I get you some refreshment?"

"No, thank you," Sister Teresa replied. "This is Friday and one of my fast days."

"But surely you eat something?" Dorinda questioned.

"As little as possible," the Sister answered. "I find that I indulge myself far too much aboard ship where meals are regular and really too plentiful as far as I am concerned."

"Do tell me about your work," Dorinda begged.

The Sister sat down on one of the comfortable chairs,

but Dorinda noticed that she sat straight and upright as if determined at all times to discipline herself.

"I have worked in the Malay Straits for twelve years," she said. "Before that I was in India."

"And you are now in Singapore?"

The Sister shook her head.

"No," she said. "I helped build up the Catholic Mission Schools in Singapore and now I have moved to Sarawak. There is a great deal to be done there. I have started not only a school for children but also a small hospital which was greatly needed."

"I thought there were Head-Hunters in Sarawak. Are you not frightened?" Dorinda asked.

Sister Teresa laughed.

"I assure you that they will not take my head," she said, "and, as I expect you know, Sarawak has a white Rajah. Sir Charles Brooke is very kind to the Missionaries and we can always turn to him in times of trouble."

"I am sorry that you will not be staying in Singapore," Dorinda said.

She thought how much Letty would miss the Sister and what a relief it would have been to know there was at least one person in the town whom she liked and trusted.

"I shall be in Singapore for perhaps two or three weeks after we arrive," Sister Teresa said, "and I must introduce you to Father Pierre Pâris who is our Catholic Priest. He is a very much-loved personality."

She smiled and added:

"Everyone in Singapore recognises the Father when he walks about with a Chinese umbrella in one hand and a stick in the other!"

Dorinda laughed.

She could imagine that a Catholic Priest in his long black cassock carrying a Chinese umbrella would look a little unusual.

"I suppose most of the children you help are Chinese?" she said.

"There are at least twenty-eight different nationalities

in Singapore," Sister Teresa answered, "but at the moment there are overy eighty-thousand Chinese, which is a great majority of the inhabitants."

"As many as that!" Dorinda exclaimed in surprise.

"Singapore is a large and growing community," Sister Teresa told her, "as you will soon see for yourself."

"I want to thank you," Dorinda said in a soft voice, "for all you have done for Lady Lettice."

She hesitated a moment and then she asked:

"Will you help me to make her realise how important it is for her to help Mr. Kirby in his work and all he is trying to do for the Colony?"

"Have you met Mr. Maximus Kirby?" Sister Teresa asked.

"No," Dorinda replied, "but I have heard a great deal about him."

"He is a very distinctive and unusual person," Sister Teresa said, slowly as if she was feeling for words. "He has a strong, decisive character and is greatly admired in Singapore."

"I have heard . . ." Dorinda began.

But as she finished speaking, Sister Teresa had risen to her feet and without saying any more was gone from the Cabin.

Dorinda stared as the door closed behind her.

She had a feeling that the Sister had spoken with intent.

Had she meant to warn her of what Maximus Kirby would expect of Letty, or had she been saying quite positively that she did not think Letty was the right person for him?

She had the feeling the ship was moving too quickly and she was being hurried towards a situation for which she was unprepared and for which she certainly had no solution.

She walked across the State-Room and very quietly opened the door into Letty's Cabin.

She was lying asleep and as Dorinda stood looking down at her she thought no-one could possibly be more exquisitely lovely.

Letty looked like the Princess in a fairy-tale with her hair spread over the pillow and falling over her shoulders. Her lashes very dark against her white skin; her mouth wistfully drooping a little at the corners, was at the same time a perfect cupid's bow.

'No-one could look more romantic, more alluring or more feminine,' Dorinda told herself.

Then she saw in her mind's eye the strangely arresting face of Maximus Kirby.

It was the face of a man of action! A man, as Sister Teresa had said, of character and personality; a man who would demand what he wanted of life and make certain that he got it!

Dorinda found herself praying that somehow Letty could bring him happiness.

Was it possible that two people from such different backgrounds, with so little in common, could make a life together?

With a deep sigh she remembered how helpless Letty was and how completely self-centered.

Dorinda returned to her cabin and picked up her book but somehow it was impossible to read.

Instead she went to the open port-hole and looked out.

The sunshine blindingly golden shimmered on the sea. It was so smooth it was hard to remember how only a short while ago they had pitched and tossed and been thrown from side to side of their Cabin.

Now there was so little wind that the sails hung limp and they had to rely solely on the engine to propel them through the water.

That evening when Sister Teresa was looking after Letty, Dorinda went up on deck.

It was fascinating to find that, though darkness had fallen, she did not need a cloak over her thin dress.

The sky was filled with stars and, though it was slightly cooler than it had been during the afternoon, it was still very hot. It was a warm moist heat which had made Letty complain fretfully for several days.

"It is always stifling in the Red Sea," Sister Teresa had said soothingly. "It will be better now we are out in the Indian Ocean."

'I like it!' Dorinda had thought.

It was the truth.

She found the hot, moist air had swept away the catarrh from which she always suffered in the winter.

She no longer felt constricted at the top of her nose nor was there a pain beneath her eye-brows. She could breathe better and it was a relief she had not expected.

"Everyone suffers from catarrh in the winter," her mother had said once, "so do not think, Dorinda, you are unusual in any way."

"I do not, Mama," Dorinda replied. "I only mentioned it as it makes me feel so stuffed-up."

"I cannot bear minor ailments!" the Countess said sharply.

Dorinda had felt hurt that her mother was so unsympathetic but in a way she could understand it.

Letty complained of the slightest thing and the Countess, who suffered twinges of rheumatism all through the winter, had her own aches and pains to endure without hearing about other people's.

Her father however had been much more understanding.

"Try a little of my snuff, Dorinda," he said. "I take it when I have a cold and it helps me considerably."

Dorinda had done what he suggested, but it had only seemed to make the congestion in her nose worse.

She had an idea it was not ordinary catarrh but perhaps part of the eczema which disfigured her face.

If that was so, she knew there was nothing to be done about it. She had long ago given up taking any remedies for her disfigurement, she knew only too well how ineffective they were.

Now looking out over the sea she drew a deep breath.

Yes, her nose was definitely much clearer.

She walked around the deck finding there were few

other people about. She heard gusts of raucous laughter from the Smoking-Saloon and knew where the passengers who had not gone to bed were amusing themselves.

She thought, listening to the masculine voices, and masculine laughter, how little she knew about men.

Yet somehow with the problems she had tried to solve in the village and from confidences she had received from among the numerous servants employed in Alderburne Park, she felt she knew a lot about human nature.

Because some people dressed more expensively and lived in a higher stratum of society, it did not make them less human.

They were born and they died. They sought for happiness in the same way as the humblest scullery-maid or the lowest paid stable-boy wanted to be happy in their lives.

Dorinda envied Sister Teresa.

Her life was dedicated to helping other people and she was, Dorinda was sure, completely and absolutely confident that in her religious faith she could find the right answer to every problem.

The faith that inspired Sister Teresa was very obvious.

One could see it in the expression of her eyes; in the way she spoke and the manner in which, when she was not reading to Letty, her fingers would feel for her rosary, Dorinda knew then she was praying.

'I am sure her prayers will help Letty,' she told herself now. 'Perhaps they will work a miracle, and she will become normal and behave like other people. Perhaps being married will change her altogether."

She tried to imagine Letty as a wife and a mother, but it was too difficult to visualise.

'I am sure everything will be all right,' Dorinda told herself reassuringly.

She knew that when she was worrying about the

future she was thinking not only of Letty's happiness but also of Maximus Kirby's.

She wanted him to be happy.

He was, she thought, a person who deserved happiness in his private life. Surely it must be hard for a man to carry so much responsibility on his shoulders without knowing that he could find some peace and relaxation in his own home?

Dorinda stood looking up at the stars and suddenly she thought how wonderful it would be if she were Letty, going out to marry the most attractive man she had ever seen in her whole life.

She knew if that was to be her future she would at this moment be sending out her thoughts to him, believing they would wing their way across the sea to where he was waiting for her.

They would already be close to each other in their minds, even while their bodies were still far apart.

She imagined herself talking with Maximus Kirby, listening to him.

Then before she could prevent it she found herself thinking of him taking her in his arms! She started away from the idea, shocked at the point to which her imagination had carried her.

'How can I even think such a thing?' she asked herself.

Then with a sad little smile, she remembered that dreams hurt no-one.

She was not being disloyal to Letty, because after all what did it matter if she thought of Maximus Kirby or if she dreamt of him?

He would never know, and when she had returned to England it was all that she would have to comfort her for the rest of her life!

'I am so lucky, so very, very lucky,' Dorinda told herself.

And she knew that nothing could prevent a surge of excitement within her and the thrill of knowing that very shortly she would see him.

He had haunted her ever since she had watched him

descend from the Phaeton in which her father had brought him to their home.

"I long to see him again!" she whispered to herself.

Then she felt as if the words took wings and sped away across the sea to where Maximus Kirby was waiting to greet Letty as his future wife.

Next morning Dorinda rose early to take her walk around the deck.

There were always noises aboard ship. Apart from the throb of the engines and the sound of the creaking masts, there were the footsteps of sailors hurrying along the deck and firm notes of command.

Often Dorinda also heard music coming from the Steerage Deck. There the passengers were herded together but now it was warm a number slept on deck at night.

Dorinda liked the noise. It was, she thought, much the same as the flutter and call of bird voices which awakened her at Alderburne Park.

Having washed, she dressed with a sense of buoyancy, eager for her walk around the deck, feeling for some reason she could not explain unusually happy and alert.

She put on one of the thinnest of her new gowns. Its white collar and cuffs were as demure as a Puritan's against the grey muslin.

There was no need to wear a cloak over it or even a shawl as she had done the last few mornings.

Already it was as hot as it had been the previous afternoon, and Dorinda knew the temperature would rise as the sun grew higher in the sky until Letty and a large number of other people would find the heat intolerable.

Dorinda fastened her gown and then sat down for a moment at the dressing-table in her cabin to tidy her hair.

It was always straight and lank and there was little she could do to improve its appearance except sweep it back tidily from her forehead, and pin it neatly at the back of her head.

It was no use trying to be fashionable like Letty who wore a soft curly fringe and her long wavy hair piled high on her head or plaited into a golden carola.

Dorinda had tried every way of making her hair wave but there was nothing she could do about it.

When she was a child her nurse had sent her to bed with muslin rags tied into tight little balls all over her head.

It had been extremely uncomfortable but she had grown used to sleeping on them. It had however all proved sadly ineffective.

Five minutes after her curled hair had been exposed to the air, it hung straight and lifeless and nothing could persuade it to be anything else.

"I always had lovely hair," the Countess would say resentfully, "and your father's hair is thick and shiny. I cannot think who you take after!"

Dorinda had no answer to this, and after a time she had ceased to struggle with her hair and merely concentrated upon keeping it tidy.

She brushed it automatically now, using her brush quickly because she wished to get out on deck.

She twisted the dark strands with both hands into a low knot at the back of her neck and pushed in the hair-pins one after another, pulling the hair back tightly from her forehead.

Then she took a quick look in the mirror to see if she was tidy, half-rising to her feet as she did so.

She looked—blinked her eyes, and looked again.

She closed her eyes, squeezing them together and opened them to stare at her own reflection.

It could not be true! There must be something wrong with the mirror!

She picked up a handkerchief that was lying on the dressing-table and rubbed the glass with it.

She looked again at her own reflection.

She thought she must be mad or dreaming! It was not herself she saw but a stranger! Who could it be?

This girl with frightened eyes in an oval face, with clear, unblemished skin?

She had a smooth forehead without a mark on it; a small straight nose between grey-green eyes which seemed at the moment almost too large for her face, they were so wide and astonished.

Her upper-lip was short above a perfectly-shaped sensitive mouth, with lips which were trembling.

With a little cry Dorinda pulled back the cuffs of her dress. She stared at her arms. The skin was white and clear. The red, disfiguring patches she had known all her life were no longer there!

They had vanished!

She picked up her skirts, pulling them up to her knees and slipped down her stockings.

Her legs were nearly clear too. There were just one or two almost imperceptible markings where the eczema had been worse. Places she had scratched because the itching had been so intolerable.

"It cannot be true!" she whispered to herself.

She drew up her stockings again and turning, ran from her Cabin, along the corridor and down the stairs to the Doctor's Surgery.

She knocked at the door. When there was no reply, she knocked again.

She knew the Doctor's Cabin lay on the other side of his Surgery, and after a moment she heard his footsteps. He opened the door.

He was in his shirt-sleeves and there was a patch of soap on one cheek, suggesting she had interrupted him in the moment of shaving.

"What is it, Miss Hyde? Is Lady Lettice . . . ?"

"I had to see you, Doctor," Dorinda said breathlessly. "Look . . . look at my face! What has happened? I do not understand!"

As she had been standing in the passage she was partially in the shadow. Now the Doctor opened the door wider and she walked into the Surgery.

He looked down into her large, frightened, anxious eyes and smiled.

"You've had a dose of better medicine than any Doctor could have given you for eczema, Miss Hyde."

"I . . . do not . . . understand," Dorinda faltered.

"It is the air, my dear," he said. "The moist, hot air works miracles, as you have just found."

"I cannot . . . believe it!" Dorinda said and now there were tears in her voice. "Is it true? Really . . . true? It has . . . gone?"

"You can look for yourself," Doctor Johnson answered. "I have seen it happen before, but usually not so effectively, nor so quickly."

"It has really gone!" Dorinda cried.

She walked across the Surgery to where on the wall there was a small mirror.

"It is true!" she said. "My face is clear and my arms . . ."

Her voice broke and the tears ran down her cheeks.

"I'm thinking those are tears of happiness," Doctor Johnson said quietly. "I did not like to mention it before, but have you had that damned affliction for long?"

"All my . . . life."

"Well it's a new life you will be starting now," the Doctor said. "Sit down, Miss Hyde. The Steward has just brought me my coffee. I'm going to pour you a cup. This sort of thing is always a bit of a shock."

"I am . . . all right," Dorinda tried to say.

At the same time she felt so weak that she sat down thankfully on the hard chair in the Surgery.

The Doctor went to fetch the tray of coffee from his cabin and collected another cup for himself from a cupboard.

As Dorinda sipped the coffee, he inspected her face.

"It is one of the best transformations I have seen," he said. "It usually takes two or three days for the climate to clear the skin."

"I was on deck for a long time last night," Dorinda suggested.

"That may be the explanation," Doctor Johnson agreed. "Well, Miss Hyde, if I may say so, you are now a very attractive young woman. That promises quite a lot of different possibilities, does it not?"

Dorinda looked at him wide-eyed.

"There'll be no reason now," he smiled, "for you to eat in your Cabin. In fact you'll find people will want to look at you, and you'll not feel uncomfortable when they do so."

Dorinda drew in a deep breath.

"I cannot . . . believe it!" she said looking down at her wrists. "Has it gone for ever?"

There was a sudden note of fear in her voice.

"That depends," Doctor Johnson replied. "For some people it returns once they are in a cold, dry climate again, but usually not with anything like its previous intensity. For some it is a complete cure. That's something you'll have to find out for yourself!"

"Supposing it comes . . . back?" Dorinda asked.

The Doctor smiled.

"Well then you'll have to spend your life in this part of the world," he answered. "And I do not mind betting, Miss Hyde, you'll have a lot of gentlemen suggesting you might do just that!"

Dorinda put down her cup.

"Thank you for being so kind . . . so understanding."

"I wondered to myself if something like this might happen," the Doctor said, "but didn't mention it because there was always the chance that it might not occur where you were concerned. Eczema is one of those unpredictable diseases to which there is no stereotyped medical answer."

"But I have found the answer to mine!" Dorinda said breathlessly.

"There's another thing which might help you," the Doctor said, "especially your hair. Take a few small spoonfuls of Olive Oil internally, and rub a little Oil into your scalp before you wash it. I've seen it make a difference."

"Thank you," Dorinda said with shining eyes. "Thank you for all you have told me. I am so happy! I cannot believe it is true! I am afraid to look in the mirror again!"

"But that is exactly what I suggest you do," the Doctor said. "Sit down in front of it and meet the new Miss Hyde; she may give you quite a surprise!"

Dorinda smiled at him a little shyly before she ran as fast as her feet would carry her back to her own Cabin.

She shut the door and then apprehensively sat down again at her dressing-table.

It was true!

The girl in the mirror had a clear skin. Clear and very white.

Dorinda had always known that the parts of her body not affected by eczema were unusually white.

One of the Doctors her mother had consulted had told her that people suffering with eczema had a particularly fine-textured skin and usually, when they are not affected by the disease, it was pale in colour and very beautiful to look at.

What made all the difference to her face, Dorinda realised, was that her eye-lids were no longer affected.

She knew now that her catarrh, which must have been a part of her condition, had made her eyes puffy and seem smaller than they really were.

She stared at her chin. It was small and round, completing the almost perfect oval of her face.

Then once again the tears were running down her cheeks and she was whispering over and over again:

"Thank you, God . . . thank You . . . thank You!"

Letty was excited and so was Sister Teresa when Dorinda went into the Cabin later and found them having breakfast.

"Oh, Dorinda, how pretty you are!" Letty exclaimed.

While Sister Teresa said:

"God has blessed you, my dear, and it has made me more happy than I can say."

A dozen times an hour during that morning, Dorinda went back to the mirror to make quite certain the eczema had not returned, and each time it seemed to her that her own reflection seemed more attractive.

She told Sister Teresa what the Doctor had suggested she should do about her hair.

"It is good advice," the Sister said. "Malayans use Oil on their hair with the result that it is thick, luxuriant and curly, and the Chinese produce the shine on theirs in the same way."

"Mine will not look very pretty in lank, greasy strands," Dorinda laughed.

"Rub a very little in with the tips of your fingers, not on the hair itself but into the scalp," Sister Teresa suggested. "That is the part that has been affected by the eczema, and now that it has gone, your hair will grow thicker."

Dorinda did as she was told and in a few days, as they moved across the ocean, it seemed to her that her hair already had more life in it. Now for the first time for years she began to try to comb it into waves.

She was far too shy to obey the Doctor's suggestion that she should have her meals in the Dining-Saloon, but she no longer shrank away from the passengers who said "good-morning" or "good-evening" to her as they walked around the deck.

Soon, so naturally that she hardly realised it was happening, people stopped and talked to her.

At first she thought it was merely because they were curious about Letty, but soon she found they wanted to talk to her about other things.

Then one lady after another asked her to tea or coffee in the Saloon and she accepted their invitations.

At the same time she felt rather guilty at being sociable without Letty.

"Do get up, Letty, and come on deck," she said. "You will enjoy walking round and seeing the porpoises bobbing about in the sea."

"It is too hot!" Letty complained.

Finally, Dorinda and Sister Teresa persuaded her to dress and walk the short distance to the deck where she could lie on a chair filled with comfortable cushions in the shade of the awning.

It was obvious that at the sight of Letty everyone on board was galvanised into curiosity.

They walked past her, turned and walked past her again, and soon those who had already spoken to Dorinda stopped to chatter.

Dorinda introduced one or two of them.

Because they were mostly older people, Letty was at her most charming.

"I hear your charge has captivated the whole ship," Doctor Johnson said to Dorinda that evening.

"Lady Lettice is much better," Dorinda said, "and now we have to get her fit before we arrive at Malacca."

"The Purser has told you that Maximus Kirby is meeting you there?" the Doctor asked.

"I hear we are to leave the ship at Malacca," Dorinda answered, "to travel in Mr. Kirby's own yacht to Singapore."

"You'll have a triumphant procession all the way!" the Doctor smiled. "And I expect when you dock it will be something like the Lord Mayor's Show."

"Oh, no!" Dorinda exclaimed in dismay.

"But of course," the Doctor said. "What else do you expect where Kirby's concerned. He's always the Showman, and I don't mind betting you, Miss Hyde, his wedding'll be like a Coronation!"

"How do you know that?" Dorinda enquired.

"I know my Max," the Doctor answered. "Never could do anything quietly! You mark my words, it'll be the finest spectacle that Singapore has ever known. I only wish I could be present!"

Dorinda felt her heart sink.

If that was what was being planned, what would Letty think about it?

Because she was so anxious, she decided to take Sister Teresa into her confidence.

"The Doctor tells me he is sure Mr. Kirby will arrange a very grand wedding for himself and Lady Lettice," she said.

"I should be surprised if it were not a magnificent occasion," Sister Teresa smiled. "It is what his Chinese friends will expect, apart from the rest of the Colony."

"But Letty . . ." Dorinda began and there was no need to say any more.

The smile faded from Sister Teresa's lips.

"I know," she said, "but I think she might enjoy it, if it is explained to her beforehand exactly what to expect. What I am sure she cannot endure, Miss Hyde, are shocks of any kind. That is what upsets her."

"You are right," Dorinda agreed.

She thought of the shock it had been to Letty when she had been kissed unexpectedly, and when her father had told her bluntly that she was to leave for Singapore in a few weeks.

There had also been the shock of saying good-bye to her parents, of being violently sea-sick in a very rough sea.

"Help me, Sister Teresa," Dorinda cried impulsively. "Will you stay with Letty until she is married? I will be going home then, and she will have to manage on her own. But until then, please stay with us. I am sure Mr. Kirby would not mind."

"Maximus Kirby and I are old friends," Sister Teresa said. "He has been very kind to me in many ways. He supported me in starting the Mission School for Chinese girls when everyone else thought it would be a failure."

"Then please stay for his sake as well as for Lady Lettice's," Dorinda insisted.

Sister Teresa smiled.

"I think that at any moment you are going to tell me it is my duty."

"It is!" Dorinda said positively. "I am sure of it!"

Every day Dorinda tried to explain to Letty how important it was she should help her husband to build up Singapore to make it a great and thriving port.

"It is of importance to the world, Letty," Dorinda said, "and it is so exciting to think you can assist in its development. Perhaps they will even put up a statue to you one day, just as I believe there is one on the water-front of Sir Thomas Raffles."

"A statue of me?" Letty asked with a gleam of interest in her beautiful eyes.

"Yes, a great, big, white statue," Dorinda answered, "and perhaps with a little parrot sitting on your fingers."

"I should like that," Letty said positively. "Sister Teresa says I shall see lots of beautiful birds in Singapore."

"There are tiny sun-birds, brilliant kingfishers, bright coloured trogons and big, plumed storks who sit on top of roofs," Dorinda told her. "I have read about them in a book."

"Lots of pretty birds!" Letty cried.

"You will be able to sit in your own garden with flowers all round you," Dorinda went on, "with the birds singing you songs from the trees. You can feed the coloured cockatoos and perhaps—although I am not sure —you will be able to keep a Bird of Paradise."

Letty clapped her hands together. Because she was interested Dorinda fetched her books from the cabin and sitting on deck in the shade read to her about the birds of Malaysia.

"I am sure that everything is going to be all right," she said to Sister Teresa when they were only a day's journey away from the Straits of Malacca.

"I am praying for Lady Lettice," Sister Teresa replied. "She is the most beautiful girl I have ever seen."

Dorinda had the feeling that Sister Teresa, like herself, was trying to sound more optimistic than she really felt, but even to each other they dared not express their doubts.

The ship stopped at Penang where they said good-bye to Lady Anson.

She was met by her husband, Major-General Sir Archibold Anson, a veteran of the Crimea, who, Dorinda learnt, was an excellent Governor and much liked.

Afterwards as they steamed down the Coast Dorinda had her first sight of Malaysia.

There were high volcanic mountains in the distance and thick luxuriant vegetation growing right down to sea-level.

When they were near enough to the shore she could

see the strange houses the Malays built for themselves in the trees.

"They do that to avoid the worst of the heat," Doctor Johnson told her. "They are sensible enough to choose fruit trees when they can, which provides them with food without the trouble of growing or buying it, as well as shade!"

Dorinda exclaimed with delight when she first saw women working amongst the trees and wearing very wide-brimmed hats.

"They are a sensible, practical race!" Doctor Johnson said. "A Chinaman usually has a very good reason for everything he does."

What struck Dorinda as they moved slowly along the Coast was the enormous number of children in such a sparsely populated part of the country.

There were Malay boys bathing in the sea and riding on the backs of buffaloes, Chinese boys and girls working with their parents in what appeared to be vegetable patches.

"For Malaysian husbands and wives, whatever their race," the Doctor explained, "it is a disaster to be childless. All the races out here have a high birth-rate and children form about forty-five percent of the population, which is a far, far higher proportion than in Britain."

"They are certainly very attractive," Dorinda said looking at the shining brown bodies, thick dark hair and wide, curious eyes.

"There is nothing so attractive to my mind as the small Chinese children," the Doctor said. "You must get Sister Teresa to show you the Mission School she started."

"She has told me about it," Dorinda said.

"That woman is a Saint, make no mistake about it," the Doctor offered. "She fights like a tiger for her children, but she puts up with incredible hardships and discomforts for herself."

"I am very grateful to you for introducing her to us," Dorinda said, "and for all the help she has given Lady Letty."

"Tomorrow we shall see exactly how effective that help has been," the Doctor said dryly.

With a little leap of her heart Dorinda remembered that tomorrow they would be in Malacca.

Maximus Kirby would be waiting for them and now for the first time, she would not be afraid to meet him. There was no reason to hide. No reason to watch him from behind the curtains or between the bannisters.

She looked a perfectly normal young woman and she could meet him on equal terms.

'And yet,' she asked herself honestly, 'is it a question of equality when I want so desperately and so irrepressibly to see him again?'

Chapter Four

"Look, Letty, look at the pretty birds!" Dorinda exclaimed and Letty gave a little cry of excitement.

It was indeed a fantastic sight and Dorinda could hardly believe that the yacht ahead of them was not a figment of her imagination.

She had expected, as had the Captain, that Maximus Kirby would be waiting for them on the Quay at Malacca, but as they steamed down the Straits and just before the small Port came in sight, they saw ahead of them a ship with pink sails.

It was, Dorinda realised with surprise, a yacht, but decorated in a manner which made it the strangest and most beautiful vessel she could have imagined.

"It is *The Sea Dragon*," she heard the Doctor snort.

She looked at him and he added in explanation which was really unnecessary:

"It belongs to Maximus Kirby. It is his Steam-Yacht!"

It was difficult to realise that it could be anything so prosaic as a ship.

The masts were festooned with pennants and the sails were a deep pink and bore the insignia of a heart surmounted by two fat cupids.

The ship itself was a bower of flowers. Superstructures had been built on either side of the funnel which was thus completely concealed, and these were covered with brilliant flowers of every description—the blossoms of Malaysia.

There were garlands of them hanging over the sides
and the railings were entwined with lianas, the rope-like
creeper which, with its crimson flowers, makes the
jungle almost impassable.

On deck at each end of the yacht were mounds of
flowers built into the shape of small patforms supporting
enormous gilded cages in which there was a profusion
of birds.

Even at the distance at which they were from the
yacht, Dorinda could see the colourful plumage of
parakeets and cockatoos.

"Parrots like mine!" Letty cried and Dorinda knew
that nothing could have pleased her more.

It was typical, she thought, of all she had heard
about Maximus Kirby, that he shoud have remembered
how pleased Letty had been with the parakeets he had
brought her in England, and now magnified his first
small gift a thousand times for her arrival.

She was to learn in a few moments that he was even
more thorough in recalling what had pleased Letty.

The Sea Dragon went ahead of *The Osaka* and led
them into the harbour of Malacca.

It was not very large and because it was obviously
too shallow near the shore for large ships, a long jetty
had been built out into the sea.

The yacht moved to the south side of the jetty and
The Osaka to the north. They tied up almost opposite
each other so that it was easy for those on board the
ship to see clearly the decorations, the fluttering birds
in their golden cages, and the pink sails slowly subsiding
now they were out of the wind.

"I told you he was unusual!" Dorinda heard a voice
say and found Doctor Johnson was standing beside her.

"It was so clever of him to think of it," she replied.

"Kirby is clever—extremely clever," the Doctor
averred.

It certainly appeared to be the truth where Letty was
concerned.

She was looking almost unbelievably lovely as she
stood at the rails of *The Osaka*.

She had also been so much better in every way, this last week, that Dorinda had begun to think that Sister Teresa's prayers and her own instructions were really beginning to work.

In fact having, as the Doctor said, captivated everybody the first day, Letty had continued to make herself so charming that Dorinda knew everyone was saying that she was exactly the right bride for Maximus Kirby.

Now, wearing one of the prettiest gowns in her trousseau, she looked every man's ideal woman.

Of very pale pink crepe, it clung very tightly, as was the fashion, to her young figure until it reached her knees, and then it frothed to the ground in small tucks to end in a slight train.

Down the front there were tiny bows of turquoise satin, and the same colour trimmed the small straw hat Letty wore on top of her shining golden hair.

In her hand she carried a minute parasol in the mode the Queen had made fashionable; an exquisite concoction of pink frills with just a touch of turquoise nestling amongst them.

At the first sight of the yacht there had been no sign of Maximus Kirby, but now as *The Sea Dragon* docked ahead of them, Dorinda saw him come on deck.

He was in white; his well-cut suit accentuated his broad shoulders, narrow waist and slim hips, but it was difficult to look at anything but his arresting face.

He was more sun-burnt than when Dorinda had last seen him, and it seemed to make his dark blue eyes even more remarkable than they had been before.

'And yet,' Dorinda asked herself, 'what woman would notice anything but the attractive twist of his lips and the expression on his face—that of a buccaneer who has just captured a prize cargo!'

The crowd which had assembled on the Quay-side were waving excitedly to *The Osaka* as she drew up to the jetty precisely opposite *The Sea Dragon*, and the anchor ran down.

Then as the gang-way was pushed into place Dorinda saw below a very strange Guard-of-Honour.

It was comprised of children, some Chinese and some Malay, and they were all wearing their National costume.

The Malayan children were dressed in little red cotton coats, knee-length over a sarong. These had been introduced by the Portuguese in the sixteenth century and were still worn automatically by every Malaysian.

The Chinese boys with long pig-tails had round scull hats and brightly embroidered coats over black trousers.

The children were small and each one of them held in his hand a litle wicker bird-cage containing a para-keet.

Then as the gang-plank was in place, Maximus Kirby left *The Sea Dragon* and walking through the excited chattering crowd came slowly up the gang-way.

He was followed by two children; one Chinese and one Malay—each carrying a bird-cage with its brightly-coloured occupant.

As he stepped onto the deck of *The Osaka,* Dorinda thought breathlessly she had forgotten how big, over-powering and attractive he was.

Bare-headed he walked directly to Letty and taking her gloved hand raised it to his lips.

"I have been waiting," he said, "for what has seemed a century for this moment when I could welcome you to Malaya."

His voice was very deep.

Letty smiled at him and it was with a feeling of relief that Dorinda realised that apparently at the moment she had no fear of her future husband.

Maximus Kirby turned from Letty to Dorinda.

"You must be Miss Hyde," he said. "The Earl told me in his cable that you had kindly consented to accompany Lady Lettice."

Dorinda curtsied.

She found it hard to look into Maximus Kirby's eyes and her lashes were dark against her cheeks as he passed on to Sister Teresa.

He held out both his hands to her.

"My most favourite—my most beloved Missionary!"

he exclaimed. "Are you still intent upon saving the souls of the Head-Hunters, instead of concerning yourself with mine?"

"I gave up yours years ago!" Sister Teresa laughed.

"I cannot tell you how kind Sister Teresa has been to us," Dorinda interposed. "She nursed Lady Lettice on the journey and we are hoping with your permission that she will stay with us until we reach Singapore."

"You will travel with us on *The Sea Dragon?*" Maximus Kirby asked. "Nothing could give me greater pleasure!"

"Thank you," Sister Teresa replied.

"There is no need to thank me," Maximus Kirby answered. "Everything I have is yours!"

It was the conventional Eastern greeting of a host to a guest, but Sister Teresa said mischievously:

"Careful! I might hold you to that!"

"I am not afraid where you are concerned!" Maximus Kirby smiled.

He put out his hand in greeting to Doctor Johnson who said:

"Miss Hyde has tried to tell you how grateful we all are to Sister Teresa. We had a very unpleasant passage through the Bay of Biscay."

"I know this means," Maximus Kirby said in mock dismay, "that I shall have to provide an endless supply of comforts for Head-Hunters who must be preserved at all costs to continue their nefarious trade!"

They all laughed, but Dorinda noticed that while everyone had crowded round Maximus Kirby, Letty was with the children who had brought her the birds.

They were so small and so pretty that Dorinda could understand her interest. At the same time she wished that Letty would give her attention to her future husband.

It was as if at the same moment Maximus Kirby himself realised that Letty was not in the admiring group clustered around him and he went back to her side.

"If you are ready," he said, "shall we go on board

my yacht? I am waiting to show you the birds I have there. I think they will please you.".

"I love birds!" Letty cried. "Can I keep all those the children have brought for me?"

"I think you will find plenty on *The Sea Dragon*," Maximus Kirby replied, "and the garden of our new house is full of them."

He offered her his arm as he spoke. Letty took it almost absent-mindedly, her eyes still fixed on the parakeets in the small cages the children carried.

Dorinda and Sister Teresa said good-bye to the Captain, Doctor Johnson and a number of the passengers.

"Do not worry," the Doctor said as he took Dorinda's hand, "I am sure everything is going to be all right. Just keep her quiet, and remember—no shocks!"

"I can never thank you enough for everything!" Dorinda told him.

"And do not forget to enjoy yourself!" he replied. "If you take my advice and remain out here I promise I shall be a frequent caller."

Dorinda smiled at him. He noticed she had a dimple at the corner of her mouth as she quoted:

"What if 'Nobody asked me, Sir, she said'?"

"There will be no question of that!" the Doctor prophesied.

Then thinking that Letty might miss her, Dorinda ran down the gang-way and across the jetty to where Maximus Kirby was helping Letty aboard.

They went at once to inspect the big, golden cages.

Never had Dorinda seen such a collection of exotic and beautiful birds, their plumage a kaleidoscope of colour.

As soon as Letty set foot on board the yacht there was the music of a band. They used native instruments, but they were playing European music.

Dorinda commented on this to Sister Teresa.

"You would not enjoy either Chinese of Malayan music," she said, "even though the Babas of Malacca are noted for being musical and for improvising words to their tunes."

"Why should I not like their music?" Dorinda asked.

"For one thing, it is very difficult to distinguish any particular melody," Sister Teresa replied. "They simply slide their fingers at random up and down the strings with a piece of iron which produces the most extraordinary sounds."

She laughed.

"A player will harp upon one string for hours playing the same note over and over again."

"It sounds rather monotonous," Dorinda said. "But they can obviously play European music very well."

"They learnt the violin from their Portuguese neighbours," Sister Teresa told her, "and they add it to their fiddles and tom-toms. They also have an instrument which makes a sound rather like the bag-pipes. It is their favourite!"

Maximus Kirby had obviously insisted that the orchestra on board *The Sea Dragon* should confine itself to waltzes and some of the opera tunes which were popular favourites in London.

Letty did not seem to hear the music. She was so intent on the birds in the golden cages.

Maximus Kirby stood beside her, and looking at them from a distance Dorinda felt it would be impossible to find a more incredibly handsome couple.

She was sure that everyone they had left behind on *The Osaka* was saying the same thing. And as *The Sea Dragon* moved out to sea, the decks of the ship were lined with passengers waving good-bye.

Dorinda and Sister Teresa waved in return, but Letty was obviously too engrossed with her birds and Maximus Kirby with her for them to notice anything else.

As it was still very early in the morning, and as the sun was not yet as hot as it would be later on, they lingered on deck for some while.

Then they went down to the big, comfortable Saloon which seemed to fill the centre of the ship, and there were punkahs like small sails moving rhythmically to keep the air cool.

There they enjoyed another breakfast, although they had already had one on *The Osaka.*

There were fruits of every sort and variety, cold drinks made of fruit juices, and small sweet-meats of which the principal ingredients were nuts and honey.

Maximus Kirby wished to hear about their journey, and while Sister Teresa related how rough the sea had been after they left Tilbury, Dorinda watched Letty a little apprehensively.

Now she was away from the birds she was not so animated as she had been when Maximus Kirby had first come on board.

Dorinda moved to her side to say:

"Did you not think the children were sweet?"

"Sister Teresa has told me about the little Chinese children," Letty answered. "I am going to see them when we get to Singapore. They are like dolls."

"Yes, you are right," Dorinda agreed. "They are like dolls."

She thought with delight that here was another interest for Letty.

When they had finished their refreshments she suggested that they should go up on deck and watch the children playing on the sea-shore as they sailed down the coast.

She had seen so many of them the previous day that she was certain there would be plenty for Letty to watch and she was not mistaken.

The Sea Dragon, could move in closer to the shore than *The Osaka* had been able to do, and now it was easy to see the details of the coastal forest which grew right down to the water.

There were mango-groves, Casuarina trees, bamboo and palms of every sort and description.

"I did not realise palms grew so tall," Dorinda remarked to Sister Teresa and did not know that Maximus Kirby was listening.

"There are a hundred and fifty different species of palm," he answered, "but here you only see some of them, such as coconut, sugar, sago, lontar and areca palms."

"They all look rather the same to me," Dorinda said.

"You will learn to be discriminating when you have been here for some time," he replied. "There are more species of trees in Malaya than anywhere in the world."

"And judging by your wonderful decorations," Dorinda smiled, "a very large variety of flowers."

"Especially orchids," he agreed. "There are innumerable different types of orchids and each in my opinion more beautiful than the last!"

"While Lady Lettice likes the birds," Sister Teresa said, "I must admit to having a great affection for the animals."

"Surely not the tigers!" Maximus Kirby exclaimed. "Or do they also find a place in your ever-open heart?"

"Not man-eating tigers!" Sister Teresa confessed. "There are far too many of those, as you well know."

"I have done my best to keep the numbers under control," Maximus Kirby answered.

"Do you shoot them?" Dorinda asked.

Sister Teresa laughed.

"You are talking to the crack-shot of Malaysia," she said. "He could carpet his house if he wished to with the skins of all the tigers he has killed."

"When I first came to this part of the world they were a real menace," Maximus Kirby said. "There was never a week and rarely a day that we did not have reports of someone being killed and children being carried away from their villages."

"It sounds rather frightening," Dorinda agreed. "At the same time tigers are very beautiful animals, and it seems sad that they should be completely exterminated."

"You need not be afraid of that at least for many years," Maximus Kirby answered. "As Sister Teresa will tell you, a Plantation Manager can sometimes get no labourers to work on his land where the tigers take too great a toll of the coolies."

"Mr. Kirby is right," Sister Teresa said. "And that

is why there is a Government reward of a hundred and fifty dollars for every dead tiger that is brought into a Police Station."

"You are making me afraid that your country is a very dangerous place," Dorinda remarked.

"You will be quite safe with me," Maximus Kirby said positively, and she felt it would be impossible not to believe and trust him.

They moved on down the coast and Dorinda heard stories of the leopards, the tapirs and the civet cats which inhabit the jungle.

But while they talked, Letty, after watching the children splashing about in the smooth sea or running down from their tree-like houses to wave at the yacht, had walked away towards one of the big bird-cages.

Dorinda hoped that Maximus Kirby would not realise that it was impossible for Letty to concentrate on one subject or to take part in a conversation for very long.

She invariably returned to what had previously interested her. At this moment she was obsessed by the birds and was not capable of listening to anything else.

As if Sister Teresa knew that Dorinda was worried, she suggested to Letty that she should wash her hands and tidy before luncheon, which was to be served at twelve o'clock.

Dorinda and Maximus Kirby remained behind on deck.

"It was most kind of you to accompany Lady Lettice on this journey," he said pleasantly.

"It is the most exciting thing I have ever done in my whole life!" Dorinda answered.

"You have not travelled before?"

"No."

"And what did you think about it?"

"I am consumed with excitement and curiosity," Dorinda answered. "It is so different from reading about a place to actually see it."

"And you have read about Malaya?"

"What I could find about it," she answered. "There

is lamentably little literature about this part of the world."

"That is true," he answered. "Perhaps, Miss Hyde, you yourself will go home and write a book about Singapore!"

"After so short a visit?" Dorinda asked. "Can you imagine the scathing remarks that would be made about my mistakes? The only person who could write adequately about Singapore would be yourself, Mr. Kirby."

"I have thought about it," he answered, "but I have not had the time."

"That I can understand," Dorinda said. "But of course you will be able to do it when you are older. I am told that is an excellent way of spending one's retirement!"

"Are you killing me off so quickly?" he asked.

She shook her head.

"I think you are too much needed here at the moment for you to die young."

"In other words you are fatalistic enough to believe that until one's job is done, one is not released into what, if the Christians are to be believed, will be a better and less troublesome world."

"You have expressed very ably what I am trying to say myself!" Dorinda smiled.

As she spoke she thought how easy it was to talk to him. It was true she found it hard to look directly into his eyes, but apart from that she did not feel shy or constrained.

She had from the Minstrel's Gallery listened to Maximus Kirby when he had stayed at Alderburne Park, and she knew how interesting he could be.

But she did not learn of his acute sense of humour until they had sat down to luncheon and he kept her and Sister Teresa laughing helplessly at his stories of the Chinese in Singapore, of the pomposity of the Government officials and the way the Chinese thieves worked.

"Their latest trick," Maximus Kirby said, "is to tie fish-hooks into their pig-tails so that anyone who tries to hold on to them as they are escaping finds it extremely painful!"

It became very obvious that Letty was not listening to anything that was said.

As if she had expended all her charm on leaving *The Osaka* and when she first arrived on the yacht, she now lapsed into one of her vacant moods.

As soon as luncheon was over, Dorinda suggested they should rest, and Sister Teresa took Letty away to her Cabin.

"There is an awning over the after-deck," Maximus Kirby said to Dorinda. "If you prefer a comfortable chair to your Cabin, you will undoubtedly find it cooler there."

Dorinda found he was right.

There was still a faint sea breeze, and with the awning stretched over the deck as a protection from the sun, it was delightful to sit with her feet up, her head against a comfortable cushion, and watch the coast-line as they moved over the smooth water.

She was too excited to sleep, and after she had been alone for about half an hour Maximus Kirby came and sat down beside her.

"May I join you?" he asked.

"Of course."

He stretched himself out in a wicker-chair ingeniously made to be almost like a small bed.

It was easy to adjust the back to be either low or high, and one's feet were supported comfortably on a rest which could be pulled out from under the chair itself.

"I am sure, Miss Hyde," Maximus Kirby said, "that you have made arrangements to stay in Singapore until after our wedding. I am persuaded that Lady Lettice would not wish you to leave before the great event!"

"I hoped you would invite me to be present."

"It is to be a ceremony which I think you will enjoy."

"Will you tell me about it?"

If it was to be as spectacular as she feared, Dorinda

knew the only hope was for her to learn every detail and prepare Letty for what was to happen.

"Lady Lettice will drive to St. Andrew's Cathedral in a Victoria I have had specially built for the occasion," Maximus Kirby began. "On the way there the hood will be closed. Drawn by six white horses with gold bridles and wearing feathered plumes, it will look very impressive."

Dorinda did not speak and after a moment he went on:

"The ceremony will of course be performed by the Bishop and there will be a choir of nearly a hundred. I only hope the Cathedral will hold all my friends."

He smiled.

"You will be interested in the Cathedral, Miss Hyde. It was built with convict labour and is one of the most splendid buildings in Singapore."

"What else will happen at the wedding?" Dorinda enquired.

"I have planned many surprises," Maximus Kirby replied, "but one thing which I know will please Lady Lettice is that when after the ceremony we come out to the Cathedral steps, five hundred white doves will be released from the tower."

"And you will both return in the same carriage?" Dorinda asked.

"Yes, but then the Victoria will be open and the hood decorated with lilies. We will drive back through the town so that everyone can see the beauty of my bride. There will be children with flowers all along the route who will throw them into the carriage, so that by the time we arrive at my house we shall be almost up to our necks in blossoms!"

"And then?"

"There will be an enormous Reception in the garden. There will be dancing and entertainments to amuse the guests besides the pleasure of looking at my very beautiful wife!"

Dorinda remembered the Doctor talking of a party that went on for three days, and felt herself shiver.

She had a feeling that Letty would never stand the strain of such a wedding.

"I have not yet finished arranging all the details," Maximus Kirby continued, "but I think I will have a fountain running with champagne, and another filled with exotic perfume extracted from Malayan flowers. A friend of mine will fly a balloon over the garden while the party is in progress and from it we will scatter gifts for everyone present."

He spoke so enthusiastically that Dorinda felt it was impossible to put into words her dismay, amounting almost to horror, at what he was suggesting.

It was, she knew by now, exactly what those he called "his Chinese" would expect to happen. It would all be great fun for the inhabitants of Singapore who wanted something to talk about and who would enjoy every moment of it.

But what about Letty?

"When you see my garden you will realise that it is a perfect place to hold such a party," Maximus Kirby was saying. "At night the flowers, trees and shrubs will be lit up. There will be lanterns round the dance-floor and what I think in England you call 'fairy-lights' to edge the paths and guide my guests to the little arbours where they can sit and hold hands."

He laughed.

"Or perhaps make more extravagant protestations of their affection for each other."

"It all sounds . . ."

Dorinda paused, searching in her mind for the right word.

". . . Magnificent!" Maximus Kirby completed the sentence. "That is what I want my marriage to be— a magnificent Marriage which everybody will remember for years to come."

While Dorinda was trying to find words to express what she really felt about his plans, he rose to his feet.

"I forgot to tell you, Miss Hyde," he said, "that tonight we are having a dinner-party. I am going to anchor the yacht in a small harbour down the coast of

Johore. I have asked the Sultan, who is an old friend, and a number of other people who live in that Province to join us for dinner. They are very anxious to meet my future wife and very honoured that they should be the first to have the opportunity to do so."

"I will tell Letty," Dorinda said and went below.

Letty was asleep and Dorinda went to the Cabin occupied by Sister Teresa and told her what Maximus Kirby had said.

"I was expecting something like this," the Sister said. "Do not worry. Lady Lettice has been so much better lately since I have explained to her that she must think about other people's happiness before her own. I have also taught her to pray."

"I thought perhaps you had done that."

"Not conventional prayers," the Sister told her, "but prayers that come from the heart. Prayers which come naturally to us all and which do not need formal words written by monks centuries ago, but which instead are spontaneous expressions of our deepest feelings."

She spoke with such conviction that Dorinda did not like to say that she had often wondered exactly what Letty's feelings were about anything except herself.

She was however so comforted by Sister Teresa's assertion that everything would be all right that she was not surprised to find when it was time to dress for dinner that Letty was in exceptionally good humour.

She had chosen a particularly pretty gown to wear of turquoise blue chiffon which swirled around her feet and which had a soft scarf of the same material draped across bare shoulders.

She looked so lovely in it that Dorinda exclaimed:

"You look more beautiful than your little birds, Letty, and that is a compliment!"

"I am a blue-bird," Letty replied, "and Sister Teresa says blue-birds mean happiness."

"They do indeed!" Dorinda agreed, "and you are going to be very happy, Letty, I am sure of it!"

Letty smiled at her.

"Why do you not wear one of my dresses now that you look pretty?" she asked.

For a moment Dorinda stared in astonishment.

It was the first time that Letty had ever thought to say such a thing, or in fact had made such an unselfish gesture.

"Thank you, Letty," she said, "it is very sweet of you to think of it, but I am dressed now and I do not want anyone tonight to notice anybody except you."

Dorinda thought as she spoke that whatever she wore people would have eyes only for Letty.

At the same time she was aware that her evening dress, grey though it might be, revealed the slim perfection of her curved breasts and small waist.

She had only two evening dresses with her and they had both been copied from one of Letty's expensive gowns which had come from Bond Street.

Dorinda's skin was very white against the shadowy grey of her gown and the condition of her hair had improved considerably in the last few weeks. Now there were lights in it which had never been there before.

The colour of her hair still remained somewhat shadowy—a colour it was difficult to define—but there was a softness and a buoyancy about it that it had never had before.

Although Dorinda still parted it in the centre and arranged it in a large chignon at the back of her head, it waved on either side of her oval forehead and no longer lay lank and lifeless.

They went into the Saloon to find the Sultan was already there and there were a number of married couples to whom Maximus Kirby introduced first Letty and then Dorinda.

Sister Teresa seemed to know them already.

They all had a great deal to say, and both the men and the women stared at Letty with undisguised admiration.

There was however one woman who, Dorinda noticed, had eyes only for Maximus Kirby.

She was the pretty young English wife of a man who

was obviously much older than herself. She had only in recent years come to Johore and, Dorinda realised, was the flirtatious kind of female who thought that every man was there to be captivated.

Except in comparison with Letty, she would have seemed extremely attractive, especially in a part of the world where there were so few women.

As the dinner progressed, Dorinda realised with amusement that she was making every effort to attract Maximus Kirby.

As her husband was of some importance she was seated on her Host's left while Letty was on his right with the Sultan of Johore next to her and Dorinda on his other side.

It was obvious by the time they had finished the first course that Letty, apart from smiling charmingly and being on her best behaviour, had little to contribute to the conversation.

The Sultan was therefore almost obliged to talk to Dorinda and she persuaded him to explain to her some of the characteristics of his Province and the reason why originally his family had moved to Malaya from India.

Whilst she was extremely interested in all he was saying, she could not help notice that the pretty woman on Maximus Kirby's left was doing everything possible to hold his attention, using every feminine trick and wile in the calendar.

Her name was Mrs. Thompson and it was obvious that Maximus Kirby was not particularly interested in what she had to say. He was therefore talking across her to the man on her other side.

The only thing Dorinda could do was to try and include Letty in her conversation with the Sultan and she did her best, although it was not easy, as she received so little response from her sister.

After what was a delicious meal with many dishes that Dorinda had never sampled before, the table was cleared away and they settled down to talk, while several of the guests began to play Backgammon.

There were card-tables, and Dorinda was amused and surprised to find that Sister Teresa was prepared to make a fourth at bridge even while she said firmly she did not play for money.

What was very obvious was the gaiety with which everyone talked and that they seemed to have an energy and a youthful exuberance about them which was not to be found in parties of the same type in England.

The explanation came when one of the women guests said to Dorinda:

"We cannot tell you what a treat this is for us. We spend months hardly seeing a friend, and then when Max turns up everything is changed. I would not have missed this evening for anything in the world!"

"What about coming up on deck to look at the stars?" she heard Maximus Kirby say quietly to Letty when everyone else seemed occupied.

"Are the birds still there?" she asked.

"They will have been lifted down from their high positions," he answered, "but they are still on deck."

"I would like to go and see them," Letty said. "You come, Dorinda. I want you to come with me."

Dorinda hesitated.

She knew that it would seem intolerable to Maximus Kirby that she should not leave him alone with his future bride. At the same time, if he tried to kiss Letty, there was no knowing what might happen.

She and Sister Teresa had not yet prepared her for that!

"Come, Dorinda, you must come!" Letty insisted.

Now there was a note in her voice that told Dorinda plainly that she did not wish to be alone with Maximus Kirby.

"You can hardly refuse such a request," he remarked with a smile, and Dorinda accompanied them onto the deck.

The stars filled the sky, looking like diamonds in a velvet setting. There was a small crescent moon and it was so unbelievably beautiful that Dorinda drew in her breath.

She walked to the railing hoping she would seem less obtrusive than she felt.

Behind her she heard Maximus Kirby say to Letty:

"I want to give you something, but I have not had the chance to do so earlier."

"What is it?" Letty enquired.

"A ring," he replied. "An engagement ring which I hope you will like."

Dorinda did not turn round but she heard Letty say: "It is very pretty. Now can I look at the birds?"

"I think perhaps you should first show your ring to Miss Hyde," Maximus Kirby suggested.

"Yes, of course," Letty agreed, and walked to Dorinda's side.

"Look, Dorinda, at my pretty ring."

She held out her hand as she spoke and Dorinda saw on her third finger there was a very large star-sapphire encircled with diamonds.

It was a lovely ring and obviously very valuable.

"When we reach Singapore," Maximus Kirby said to Letty, "I have for you the necklace and bracelet to match."

Dorinda realised that Letty was not listening.

"Is not that exciting?" she said. "I know you are finding it hard to thank Mr. Kirby sufficiently for such a wonderful present."

She pressed Letty's hand as she spoke and her sister understood what she was trying to say.

"Thank you very much," she said conventionally. "It is a splendid present. Now can I see the birds?"

She moved away across the deck followed by Maximus Kirby and for a moment they were out of earshot.

Dorinda stood looking at the sky and the trees surrounding the little harbour, but she did not see their beauty.

How soon would it be, she wondered, before Maximus Kirby began to realise that Letty was never interested in any of the things one expected?

They did not stay long on deck but went down below and Dorinda realised with relief that Sister Teresa, knowing that Letty was tired, took her away to bed.

Because she was embarrassed that her sister should withdraw from the party that had been given in her honour, Dorinda exerted herself to be charming to everyone.

She listened to everything they had to tell her, laughed at their jokes and tried for the first time in her life to be a Hostess.

If it had not been for Letty and her anxiety about her, she would have enjoyed herself enormously.

It was the sort of party, informal and gay, in which she had always imagined taking part, but had known, because of her appearance, she would never have the opportunity.

Now that Letty was no longer there to dazzle their eyes, the men paid her compliments and the women, because they did not need to feel particularly jealous of her, chatted away confidentially as if she was one of themselves.

It was with a sense of surprise that Dorinda realised it was long after midnight and the Sultan rose to go. Regretfully the rest of the party knew they must follow suit.

"It has been a great pleasure to have Your Highness with us," she heard Maximus Kirby say to the Sultan.

"Next week I am going to give a party for you and your beautiful bride," the Sultan replied. "When is the wedding?"

"In two weeks' time," Maximus Kirby answered.

Dorinda felt as if he had struck her a blow.

Only two weeks in which to prepare Letty for what lay ahead and for her only two more weeks in this new and enchanting world!

While the Sultan and the majority of the guests were making their farewells, there were two men engrossed in a game of Backgammon.

"I can't leave yet, Max!" cried Mr. Thompson, the man with the pretty wife. "I've just lost thirty pounds and I'm determined to win it back."

"There is no hurry, as you well know," Maximus

Kirby replied. "The night is still young and it is far too early for any of us to go to bed."

"That's true," another man said, "and if you're going to stay, Thompson, Bill and I will have a game and the winner will challenge the winner of yours. Do you agree?"

"I agree!" Mr. Thompson answered, and his opponent assented.

Having said good-bye to the Sultan, Dorinda went to Letty's Cabin to find she was asleep. When she looked in on Sister Teresa it was to find that she had already undressed and was preparing to go to bed.

"Are they still here?" she asked Dorinda.

"Some of them."

"Then do not worry about us. Go and enjoy yourself, child. I could see how happy you were this evening."

"I was," Dorinda answered.

She went back into the Saloon.

She watched the men playing Backgammon, then thinking perhaps they did not like people staring over their shoulders, she slipped up the companion-way.

She wanted to go outside and look at the beauty of the night; to stare at the jungle and think how mysterious it was.

She came out on deck.

It was very quiet and she was just going to cross to the railing when she saw the flutter of a light dress and realised she was not alone.

Standing under the awning in the bow of the ship there were two people.

Dorinda hesitated.

Should she join them, she wondered? If she did so, she was certain that Mrs. Thompson, for that was who was there, would think she was intruding.

Then as she tried to decide what she should do, she saw Mrs. Thompson put her arms around Maximus Kirby's neck and draw his head down to hers.

He held her close, and now unable to move, Dorinda realised he was kissing her.

She had never seen a man kissing a woman passionately before. There was something in the locked figures, in Mrs. Thompson's hands on Maximus Kirby's broad shoulders, in her fair head close against his dark one, which made Dorinda feel very strange.

She could not explain to herself what she did feel.

It was one thing to think about two people embracing each other, quite another to see it happening and some detached part of her mind told her that Maximus Kirby showed an expertise in what he was doing now as he had in everything else.

There was a grace about his figure and the angle of his head so that she knew that his kisses would be different from those of other men . . .

Then it occurred to her that she was spying on him; that he would think it impertinent and intrusive if he knew that he was being watched.

Slowly, conscious that she ought to feel shocked or disgusted, but aware only that she felt something very different, Dorinda returned to the Saloon.

The game had just finished. Mr. Thompson was paying his opponent and the other two men had abandoned their game and were drinking whisky out of long glasses.

"It is time we left," Mr. Thompson said, "otherwise I am certain our voices will keep Lady Lettice awake."

"I have to be up at dawn," his opponent remarked. "I keep my late nights for Saturday."

Someone made a remark that Dorinda did not catch but it made them all laugh uproariously, and it was at that moment that Mrs. Thompson, followed by Maximus Kirby, came back into the Saloon.

His expression was enigmatic and Dorinda thought there was a slightly cynical twist to his mouth but there was a light of triumph in Mrs. Thompson's blue eyes and her lips were provocative.

'It was what she intended all the evening,' Dorinda thought. 'She has got what she wanted and it pleases her!'

Everybody said their last good-nights and expressed their thanks. Then they were being rowed ashore to where Dorinda knew there were horses and carriages awaiting them, or perhaps hired rickshaw boys to carry them back to their Plantations.

She stood at the railing watching the boat with a lantern on the stern receding into the darkness.

Mrs. Thompson was waving, raising her white arm until they were finally out of sight.

Then there was just the flicker of lights amongst the trees, not as brilliant as the stars above nor the moon that was growing brighter as it crept up the sky.

It was so lovely and there was something so magical about it all that Dorinda forgot for a moment that she was not alone.

And then she heard Maximus Kirby with a note of amusement in his voice say:

"I am waiting!"

Chapter Five

"Waiting?" Dorinda repeated in surprise. "For what?" what?"

"For the lecture you are obviously going to give me!"

Dorinda did not answer and Maximus Kirby continued mockingly:

"Surely it is your duty as a Chaperon to rebuke me, or can you really be so banal as to say that you—'leave it to my conscience'?"

"It is not for me either to criticise or rebuke you, Mr. Kirby."

There was a little pause and then he asked:

"Are you shocked?"

The tone of his voice had now changed and she answered him seriously:

"I do not really know . . . I do not think I am shocked . . . I think I . . . understand . . ."

She saw him smiling in the moonlight and thought he had the same cynical twist on his lips that she had noticed when he came back to the Saloon.

She knew that he was waiting for her to say more, and somehow she felt compelled, in a manner she did not understand, to tell him what was in her mind.

"I remember," she began slowly, "years ago my father went with a friend of his, a somewhat raffish Peer, to the Derby race meeting. The Peer made a great deal of money and when my father drove him home in his Phaeton, he started throwing all the silver he had in his pockets as well as sovereigns and half-sovereigns

to the crowd. It caused a commotion and my father said
to him:

" 'Why are you doing that?'

" 'They want it and I have it,' he answered."

Dorinda did not look at Maximus Kirby while she
was speaking. Instead she stared straight ahead at the
silhouette of the mountains and the forests against the
sky.

"So you think I am being generous with my kisses?"
Maximus Kirby remarked. "You are a very unusual
person, Miss Hyde."

She thought he was laughing at her.

"I do not know why you should say that."

"I have the feeling," he said, "but I cannot explain
it to myself, that you are not quite what you appear to
be—the grey dress, the demure appearance perhaps
hides something quite different."

Dorinda was silent.

'He is too perceptive,' she thought and yet she was
surprised that he had even noticed her.

"Have you ever been kissed?" Maximus Kirby asked
unexpectedly.

Dorinda felt the colour come into her cheeks and
hoped that as it was dark he would not see.

"That is not the sort of question you should be
asking me, Mr. Kirby," she replied in what she hoped
was a repressive tone.

"Can Englishmen be as cold-blooded as they are
reputed to be?" he asked, "or are you as austere as the
colour in which you dress?"

"I think I should . . . retire," Dorinda said in a low
voice.

"I am almost convinced," Maximus Kirby went on
as if she had not spoken, "that underneath that puri-
tanical appearance there is a warm heart and perhaps
a fire that no-one has yet ignited. I would like to know
the reason why."

"We were talking about you, Mr. Kirby, not about
me!"

He gave a little laugh.

"I told you, Miss Hyde, that you were different from other women. I have never yet met a woman who did not wish to talk about herself."

"That must generally involve talking about you," Dorinda said quickly and wished she could have taken back the words as soon as she had spoken them.

Again Maximus Kirby laughed.

"So you have a temper too! I am beginning to learn quite a lot about you, Miss Hyde!"

"I doubt if you will find me very interesting," Dorinda said in a voice which she tried to make indifferent, "and anyway there is very little time if you are to be married in two weeks, for I shall then be returning to England."

He did not speak. Although he had not moved she had the feeling that somehow he had come nearer to her.

Her heart was beating unaccountably in her breast and, because the exchange of words was stimulating, she felt a strange excitement she had never known before.

"I have always trusted my intuition in everything I have ever done," Maximus Kirby said after a moment, "and at this moment my intuition, for no reason I can possibly ascertain, tells me that I should somehow prevent your return. But why it should tell me that, I have no idea."

"That will give you something to puzzle about, but I think you will find no answer," Dorinda said lightly.

As she spoke she realised that as they had been talking the tide had swung the yacht so that they were no longer looking into the small harbour but instead faced the open sea of the Straits.

It was then she saw coming towards them several ships with square mainsails.

They were strangely shaped and she remembered that the Doctor had told her that such sails, made of kajang, were stitched on to bamboo spars and hoisted on a tripod bamboo mast.

She saw the small ships without really thinking about

them, but considering what next she should say to Maximus Kirby.

She wanted to go on talking to him, and yet she knew that if she behaved correctly she would go below to her Cabin.

Yet one part of her brain watched the ships coming nearer and now she saw that they were not relying on the wind but were being rowed, and there were perhaps nine oars on each side.

"I thought there could not be enough breeze at the moment for those ships to move so quickly," she remarked.

Maximus Kirby turned his head to look out to sea.

He stared for a moment and then he was suddenly tense.

"Prahus!" he exclaimed.

"You mean they are pirates?" Dorinda asked.

He did not answer. Instead he pulled her away from the rail and drew her across the deck to the companion-way.

"Go below!"

It was a command, but as Dorinda stood irresolutely in the shadow of the deck-house, he disappeared, and she looked back to where the prahus were still drawing nearer to the yacht.

She tried to remember all that she had been told about the pirates and remembered that they carried guns on their ships.

She did not feel frightened. Somehow it did not seem real, six prahus coming swiftly upon them and making no noise. There was not even any splash of oars as they rhythmically moved in and out of the still water.

Then as she stood in the shadow of the door that opened onto the deck, she realised there was activity all round her.

Men lying absolutely flat were crawling along the deck in every direction.

She realised they were protected from the view of the approaching prahus by the thick ropes of lianas twisted round the railings.

From where she stood she could also see one platform
of flowers on which had rested the huge gilt bird cage
containing the parrots and cockatoos.

It had, as Maximus Kirby told Letty, been lifted
from its place just in case, Dorinda supposed, a wind
should spring up unexpectedly during the night and it
might be upset.

The cage had been placed securely against the centre
superstructure but now she could see hands were swiftly
stripping the platform of flowers to reveal guns.

'They will be mounted on a swivel,' she thought, 'so
that the pirates can be fired upon whichever side of the
ship they approach.'

She remembered how the Doctor told her that the
usual practice when pirates found a ship at anchor in a
secluded harbour was for them to creep on board and
brutally massacre the passengers and crew.

On this occasion, she could see, they would have a
surprise, for the deck was covered with men.

Those that were nearest to her she could see had in
their hands krises, the short swords with wavy blades
and cockatoo hilts which Chinese had used for genera-
tions.

The first prahu had already reached the yacht and
now Dorinda could see that the top of its sail was level
with the decorated railing.

Then there was another and another and she guessed
that three ships had gone to one side of *The Sea
Dragon* and three to the other.

But still there was no sound!

It was the most uncanny thing she had ever known
that ships containing a large number of men could come
so close and yet, if she had been asleep, she would never
have heard them.

It was then she heard steps coming up the companion-way behind her and knowing who it was she
squeezed herself even closer into the shadows so that
she would not be seen.

It was Maximus, and he was in his shirt-sleeves and
held a pistol in his right hand and a kris in the other.

He stepped out on deck.

"Fire!" he shouted.

His voice seemed louder and more frightening because of the silence which preceded it.

Then all hell broke loose!

Even as Maximus Kirby spoke, heads had appeared over the ship's rail as the pirates attempted to scramble on board.

Dorinda could see them quite clearly in the moonlight. Their hair was long and she was to learn later that they let it loose in battle to increase their ferocious appearance.

They swung themselves over the rail, and she could see that they carried bamboo shields besides being armed with spears and krises.

Some had muskets but in the confusion they fired them wildly without taking aim.

Those who reached the deck were driven backwards to fall wounded or dead into the sea, and it seemed to Dorinda that in the mêlée of the fight Maximus Kirby was everywhere!

He had apparently fired all the bullets from his own pistol and now he had his kris in his right hand driving it into one pirate and then another.

Soon there were bodies dead and bloody lying all over the deck and the surviving pirates were trying to retreat, frantically rowing away from the yacht they had approached so confidently.

It was then the guns which had been concealed by the flowers fired accurately and lengthily so that the prahus sank one after the other.

They fired a few shots in return, but it was obvious that their gunners were demoralised and most of the shots went wide.

One or two reached their mark and the yacht rocked a little, but their guns were not capable of doing the same damage as Maximus Kirby's armament.

Five prahus were sunk within a few minutes of opening fire and Dorinda could see a number of the men who had manned them swimming towards the shore.

One prahu almost reached the open sea in safety before it was disabled by an accurate shot which seemed to heave it almost out of the water before it turned turtle, and its crew was abandoning it like rats.

It was all so fantastic, so unreal, that Dorinda did not feel any fear until it was all over.

Then as the shooting died away and Maximus Kirby's crew stood looking down on the dead bodies lying around them, Dorinda came from her hiding place.

"You have done well!" she heard Maximus Kirby say to his men. "I am proud of you!"

They were all Chinese and Malayan with the exception of the Captain, who was an Englishman, and they grinned at him delightedly.

He looked from his men towards Dorinda.

She thought he was about to reprimand her for not following his orders, but she saw there was a great patch of blood on his shoulder where his white shirt had been torn by a sword thrust.

"You are hurt!" she exclaimed.

As she spoke she heard Letty screaming.

It was very hot and Dorinda stood on deck watching the coastline slipping past them. It was hard to believe that what had happened last night had not been a figment of her imagination.

When she had risen this morning, having slept soundly, when she had not expected to be able to do so, every evidence of the battle had been removed.

The bodies had vanished, the deck scrubbed clean, and she had an idea that new flowers had been added to the decorations to replace those that had been damaged.

However, Maximus Kirby was wearing a bandage round his upper arm and Sister Teresa had insisted on him having his arm in a sling to prevent further bleeding. This was the only evidence that the pirates had ever attacked them.

Also a number of the crew had sword cuts on their

faces and Sister Teresa and Dorinda had bandaged the wounds on their heads and arms.

"There is no need for you to do this, Miss Hyde," Maximus Kirby had said sharply as he found her staunching a deep sword thrust.

She had raised her head from where she knelt on the deck to smile at him.

"What do you expect me to do?" she asked. "Sit in the Saloon and ring for a cool drink?"

She spoke sarcastically. He made no reply but only said to the Chinese she was treating:

"You were very brave, my lad!"

Dorinda saw a look of adoration in the dark slit eyes before Maximus Kirby moved away.

The yacht itself had not suffered except for two holes above the water-line which would have to be repaired and repainted when they reached harbour.

Otherwise there was no doubt that the pirates had been taught a severe lesson. They would be careful on another occasion not to be so stupid as to attack any ship belonging to Maximus Kirby!

"They were of course deceived by the fact that they could not see the funnel," Mr. Kirby said. "They were Sarebus pirates who have been very active round Java's coastline and must have thought we had relaxed our vigilance in the Singapore area."

The real damage that the battle had done, Dorinda and Sister Teresa knew, was to Letty.

The gun-fire had terrified her and she had screamed for a long time after the battle was over. In fact they could not stop her until Sister Teresa gave her some herbs to make her sleep.

Dorinda made no attempt the following morning to persuade Letty to get up. When she went into her Cabin, Letty was heavy-eyed, and said in a low, hesitating tone:

"I want . . . to go . . . home, Dorinda. I do not . . . like it out . . . here."

"Now, Letty, you must not be upset about what happened last night It was something no-one expected because Mr. Kirby has almost eradicated the threat of piracy around Singapore."

"I heard . . . them! I heard the . . . pirates!" Letty replied. "They were trying to . . . kill us."

"There was no chance of their doing that," Dorinda said positively, "not with Mr. Kirby to defend us. He fought very bravely, Letty, you must be proud of him."

"I want to . . . go home," Letty said stubbornly.

Dorinda knew it was no use arguing with her sister at the moment, and hoping she would go back to sleep, she went up on deck determined to put a bright face on Letty's condition as far as Maximus Kirby was concerned.

"I am afraid Lady Lettice is rather upset," she replied in answer to his enquiries. "It was more frightening for her to be down below than it was for me, because I could see what was happening."

"Which you had no right to do," he said sternly. "I gave you an order and I expect people to obey me when they are under my command!"

"You sound very ferocious!" Dorinda smiled. "Do you realise how lucky it was that we were on deck?"

"If we had not been, there would have been someone on guard," Maximus Kirby replied. "They come on duty when I have gone to bed."

He saw the argument on Dorinda's lips and said:

"You are quite right! In future there will be a watch from the moment it is dark, but I assure you that such an occurrence is not likely to happen nowadays, except perhaps once in a hundred voyages!"

"It is just unfortunate Lady Lettice should have been present this time."

As there was no answer to this Maximus Kirby did not reply.

They sailed on down the coast.

Dorinda learnt that they would reach Singapore later in the afternoon, and she was glad for Letty's sake they were not to spend another night on board.

At the same time, she was as the day passed extremely perturbed about her sister. Letty persisted in her assertion that she wished to go home.

She was also in an extremely nervous condition, trembling and clinging to Sister Teresa, and starting at every sound. It was obvious that all the good that had been done in the last week or so was now disastrously undone.

Dorinda was determined that Maximus Kirby should not see Letty in such a state. She also decided that she must beg him to be very gentle and understanding in his treatment of her sister.

Anyway she had meant to speak to him before the marriage as her father had asked her to do.

But because she was afraid that he might attempt to kiss Letty or might frighten her in some manner before she had become acclimatised to the life in Singapore, Dorinda felt it was essential she should talk to him at once.

The opportunity came in the afternoon when Sister Teresa went below to be with Letty, and Dorinda once again settled herself under the awning on deck.

She was alone for a little while, then Maximus Kirby came to join her.

He stretched himself out on a deck-chair.

"How is your arm feeling?" she enquired.

"It is only a scratch!" he answered. "Sister Teresa is making far too much fuss about it. Like all women, she likes to have a man at her mercy!"

"That is usually I believe what women say about men," Dorinda remarked.

He looked at her with a twinkle in his eye and she said in a low voice:

"I want to . . . speak to you about Lady Lettice."

"She is very distressed?"

"It was such a shock," Dorinda answered. "Having lived a very quiet life in England, Lady Lettice is not used to shocks of any sort."

There was a pause then not looking at Maximus Kirby she said in an embarrassed voice:

"I want to ask you before you . . . marry Lady

Lettice, to be very . . . gentle and . . . patient with her."

"Are you telling me, Miss Hyde, how I should make love to my wife?" Maximus Kirby enquired.

Dorinda blushed and now there was no hiding the colour which rushed into her cheeks.

"No! Of course not!" she answered uncomfortably. "I was only . . . trying to explain that Lady Lettice's attitude to . . . marriage is . . . different to that . . . of most women."

She sounded somewhat incoherent even to herself and Maximus Kirby asked:

"Are you endeavouring to convey to me, Miss Hyde, that Lady Lettice did not wish to marry me?"

There was a little pause before Dorinda said hastily:

"No . . . no, of course not. It is just that she is a long way from . . . home, and she does not . . . know you well. She had only seen you the two nights you stayed at Alderburne Park."

"I thought from what her father said to me," Maximus Kirby said, "that the idea of being my wife met with her approval."

If Dorinda had not been so worried, she would have been amused to realise that it was perhaps the first time in Maximus Kirby's life that a woman had not been ready to throw herself into his arms almost before he asked it of her.

"I am sure . . . everything will be all right," Dorinda said. "If you are patient . . . if you make her . . . fond of you before . . ."

"I understand exactly what you are trying to say to me, Miss Hyde," Maximus Kirby said sharply.

Then he rose from the chair in which he had been sitting and walked away.

Dorinda looked after him in dismay.

Had she made things worse or better, she wondered. Had she made a mistake in speaking at all? Had she perhaps put the idea into his head that things were not what he had anticipated before he found out the truth for himself?

There was no chance for further conversation.

Late in the afternoon Singapore came in sight, and while Dorinda would dearly have loved to watch the ship come into what she had learnt was the most beautiful, spacious harbour in the world, she had to help Sister Teresa.

It was a difficult task to persuade Letty to get dressed and even more difficult to persuade her to be pleasant and to look forward to what lay ahead.

It was only just before they docked that Dorinda was able to go up on deck and to see the harbour and the hundreds of ships moving towards or from the Port or at anchor in the sunlit water.

Her only consolation for missing so much was that Letty looked absolutely beautiful in a dress of white muslin, trimmed with pink ribbons. She wore a broad-brimmed hat on her head encircled with a wreath of roses.

There was a look of irrepressible admiration in Maximus Kirby's eyes as he raised Letty's hand to his lips.

"I hope you are better," he said. "I deeply regret that you should have been disturbed last night."

"I do not like the sea . . . it is . . . frightening," Letty said petulantly.

"We are just going ashore," he said, "and there will be no need for you to go to sea again for a long time."

Letty did not answer. It was obvious to Dorinda that she wanted only to get away from the ship and everything in it that had frightened her.

Dorinda shook hands with the Captain and said good-bye to some of the crew. But Letty stood pouting and obviously waiting impatiently for the ship to reach the Quay-side and for the gang-plank to be put into place.

Maximus Kirby helped her down it and they walked to where there were two carriages waiting.

Both were extremely elegant with frilled cotton awnings to keep off the sun.

Dorinda knew without being told that Maximus Kirby

had intended that he and Letty would go in one carriage and she and Sister Teresa in the other.

But Letty had no intention of being parted from either of them.

"Will you come with me?" Dorinda heard Maximus Kirby say to Letty with a smile that she felt would have made most women walk bare-footed to Tibet.

"I want to drive with Dorinda and Sister Teresa," Letty replied. "I want . . . them with me."

Maximus Kirby gave in with good grace and they travelled four in the first carriage in which, as it happened, there was plenty of room.

Dorinda had her first sight of the Town and found it as fascinating as she had expected it to be.

The streets were narrow, the houses high, sign-boards almost touching each other were hung on iron rods and hooks. They were all painted red or black with Chinese characters in gilt on them.

The fronts of the shops were embellished by strips of red paper inscribed with what Sister Teresa told her were flowery passages from the Classics.

It was amusing to see the Chinese taking tiny steps in their thick solid shoes, their hands hidden in the long sleeves of their coats or carrying a big umbrella.

The women had silver and gold pins in their hair and their faces were painted white or red.

The Chinese looked rich and prosperous, but the Malayans were often in rags and seemed to be performing the more menial tasks, such as sweeping away the dirt of the streets, cleaning the fronts of the shops or carrying great baskets or boxes on their heads.

It was difficult to get more than a quick impression because the horses travelled swiftly up the streets rising to where there were better class houses, some of them extremely impressive both in architecture and in situation.

Then at almost the top of a hill with a magnificent view over the harbour they reached Maximus Kirby's house.

Dorinda's first impression was one of delight because

the roof was covered with jade-green tiles and at the corners in Chinese fashion there were beautifully carved porcelain dragons.

There was a huge portico over the front door so that they could alight under cover, protected at all times from either sun or rain and there was a long flight of low steps.

Dorinda had not quite known what she expected. Certainly nothing so beautiful or so unique as the house Maximus Kirby had built for Letty.

It was very cool and after the bright sunshine outside it seemed almost dark when they entered an enormous room.

Then as Dorinda's eyes adjusted themselves, she saw there were treasures of every description—huge Chinese vases; inlaid furniture; pictures that Maximus Kirby must have brought from Europe; and everywhere sprays of orchids of every colour.

It was so lovely that Dorinda found herself staring round her almost rudely until she heard Letty say in a querulous tone she knew so well:

"I want to lie down . . . I feel ill."

"Yes, of course," Dorinda answered. "I am sure someone will show us the way to the bed-rooms."

The bed-rooms were in fact as elegant as she might have expected from first sight of the room downstairs. They were not over-furnished but very comfortable and Letty's room was decorated with a Chinese wallpaper of pink flowers and a profusion of exotic birds.

"Look, Letty, more pretty birds!" Dorinda exclaimed.

But by this time Letty was past being appeased by birds or anything else.

"I am . . . ill. I want to go home . . . back to England."

She repeated the words parrot-fashion over and over again, until Dorinda felt she could bear it no more.

Finally when Letty was undressed and in the big bed with white mosquito-netting draped around its canopy giving it a fairy-like appearance, Sister Teresa gave her something to drink which Dorinda knew would send her to sleep.

"I do not approve of drugs of any sort," Sister Teresa said to Dorinda when they had left the bed-room. "But this is a very mild one, and what else can I do?"

"What indeed?" Dorinda asked. "It is a tragedy that we should have been attacked last night when Letty was in such a good humour and even looking forward to seeing the house and the garden."

"Has she always been like this?" Sister Teresa asked.

Dorinda hesitated for a moment and then she told the truth.

"Sometimes she is better than at others," she answered, "but as you have seen, she finds it very difficult to concentrate on anything for long, and it is only little things that amuse her, like birds and dolls."

"And yet her father thought her suitable to marry a man like Maximus Kirby!" Sister Teresa exclaimed.

Dorinda did not reply because she knew there was nothing she could say.

She felt uncomfortable and apologetic when she and Sister Teresa joined Maximus Kirby for dinner.

He was a considerate Host, but at the same time because Dorinda was sensitive to other people's feelings she was well aware that he was surprised by Letty's behaviour.

She therefore tried in every way she could to make up for her sister's deficiencies.

Sister Teresa excused herself when dinner was over and said she wished to attend to Letty and would then retire.

Maximus Kirby made no effort to persuade her otherwise and she went upstairs, leaving Dorinda standing in the huge sitting-room in the centre of the house. She had learnt by now that nearly every other room opened out of it.

She walked across to the windows at the far end. Already it was dark, but when they had first arrived she had received a quick impression of trees and shrubs covered in brilliant blossoms and a profusion of orchids.

"It is too late now to see anything outside," Maximus Kirby remarked beside her. "Would you like to see the rest of the house?"

"I would love to," Dorinda said enthusiastically.

She hoped that her interest would in some way compensate for the fact that Letty was not with him.

She knew how disappointed she would have been if she had built anything so tremendous as a house for someone and then, when they arrived, they did not deign to notice it!

The house had many Chinese features, but it also incorporated much of the luxury of houses in England such as bathrooms and an up-to-date kitchen.

Nothing could have been more lovely than the court-yards which would be cool in the heat of the day and in which fountains played into carved stone-basins.

Above the court-yards there were covered balconies on the first floor onto which the bed-rooms opened and every room was decorated with art treasures worthy of a museum.

Dorinda had somehow not expected Maximus Kirby to have such good taste. This was an aspect of his character she had not considered.

Gorgeously decorative effects through the use of ancient tiles, sculpture and Chinese carvings gave the architecture an unusual distinction, and the furnishings themselves, the pictures, the ornaments, and carpets had obviously been collected over the years.

Finally Dorinda found as they went from room to room that the new house adjoined part of an older one.

"I bought a house on this site when I first came to Singapore," Maximus Kirby explained. "Although I pulled down a great deal of it I have kept certain rooms intact."

There was something about the way he spoke that told Dorinda that those rooms were rather special.

"May I see them?" she asked.

She fancied that he hesitated a moment before he replied:

"If it pleases you."

They went from the large, westernised version of a Chinese building into one that was small and old.

Here the rooms that remained were built around a small court-yard. There was a magnolia tree in bloom, but the rest of the shrubs that decorated it were miniatures.

Dorinda knew the little trees might be centuries old and she would have liked to examine them by the lanterns which swung from iron poles, but Maximus Kirby led her into a room which she realised at once contained many of his personal treasures.

There were Chinese bronzes so ancient that they dated back to the thirteenth century B.C., and a collection of jade which made her exclaim in delight.

"Do you know anything about jade?" Maximus Kirby asked.

"I have read that the Chinese believe it is a product of Heaven and highly charged with creative force," Dorinda answered.

"That is true," he said. "It is also supposed to have mysterious powers of healing the body and even conferring immortality."

Dorinda picked up a piece of jade which was as green as the sea had been early in the morning.

"I like to remember," she smiled, "that jade expels evil thoughts from the mind."

"Do you believe that?" he asked.

"I want to believe it," Dorinda replied. "Perhaps one day I shall have a piece of jade of my own then everytime I think something which is wrong, I shall touch it and send the thought from me."

She had spoken without considering to whom she was speaking and fearing her words would sound as if she were asking him to give her a present, she went on quickly:

"I notice another room beyond this one. May I see it?"

Again she thought that Maximus Kirby hesitated until without speaking he drew aside the embroidered hanging which took the place of a door and Dorinda found herself in a very strange room.

It was completely Eastern with cushions on the floor instead of chairs and only a few pieces of Chinese porcelain on low tables. Dorinda looked at them and gave a cry of sheer joy.

One of the figures was a Chinese horse in a warm red bronze and orange which she recognised.

"It is Täng, is it not? One of the guardians of a tomb!"

"How do you know that?" Maximus Kirby enquired.

"I have read about them," Dorinda answered, "and I wanted so much to see one."

She touched the horse with the tips of her fingers stroking its beautiful arched neck.

"Look at its tension and vigour," she said almost to herself. "It seems almost to move."

Maximus Kirby did not answer. Instead he said:

"I want you to look at my pictures and tell me what you think of them."

It was with difficulty that Dorinda raised her eyes from the horse and the other beautiful pieces of pottery.

Then she saw that hanging on the walls were three long, scroll-like pictures which she knew without being told were of great antiquity. They were sketchily painted in brush-work almost without colour.

The first picture showed flowers beside a still pool. Above them rose a great, barren crag, bleak and rough. On the very top of it was a tree blown by the wind, its branches seeming too fragile to withstand the force of it.

Dorinda stood looking at it for a long time before Maximus Kirby asked softly:

"What do you see?"

"I know," she answered, "that the Chinese painted what lay behind the world we see, the spiritual beyond the material."

She paused to say very slowly:

"I think the flowers and pool depict our existence, peaceful and commonplace."

"Go on . . ."

She thought the expression in his eyes showed surprise.

"I may be quite wrong," she said, "but I feel that, instead of staying quietly by the flowers and the pool, we are meant to . . . climb to the top of the crag. It is hard and difficult and the blustery wind may be cold and rough, yet only in this way, can we . . . develop and fulfil ourselves."

There was silence and Dorinda felt in some inexplicable way she and Maximus Kirby were very close.

Then he put out his hand, taking her arm to draw her to the other wall, where again there hung a single picture.

"Tell me what this means."

She felt herself quiver because he was touching her. She felt, although he only touched her arm, that he almost took possession of her.

There was something so magnetic and vital about him that quite suddenly she felt weak and dependent. She wanted to lean against him and know that he protected her.

He took his hand away and she forced herself not to think of him but of the picture.

Here again the artist seemed to have used as few brush strokes as possible, and yet what he had drawn had a depth behind the first impression.

The picture showed a bridge with a river flowing swiftly beneath it.

'The stream of life!' Dorinda thought to herself.

There were flowers, a tree full of fruit, and above it a cloud. Above again there were the high, pointed peaks of a mountain, glowing brilliantly white either from sunshine or snow.

They held the eye until one looked again at the flowing stream and the bridge which crossed it.

"What do you think it means?" Maximus Kirby asked.

"I am not quite . . . sure," Dorinda answered, "and

I expect it means different things to different people. It makes me feel what I cannot put into words."

She hesitated and then said:

"Perhaps I can come again to look at it until I am sure what message it has for me."

He did not reply.

She looked round the room and felt it had a strangely peaceful and quiet atmosphere.

"I am sure," she said slowly, "that you come here when you are worried or perturbed. I think this is the heart of your house."

Even as she said it, the words sounded exaggerated and un-English. Yet they had come to her lips without her really considering them.

She thought Maximus Kirby might laugh. Instead he led the way back from the ancient, Chinese part of the house to the new additions he had just completed.

Dorinda thought that he might ask her to sit down so that they could continue their talk. But instead he led her to the bottom of the stairs and she knew he expected her to go to bed.

She held out her hand.

"Good-night, Mr. Kirby. Thank you very much indeed for showing me your beautiful house."

"I am glad you admire it," he said conventionally.

There was an expression on his face she did not understand.

She wondered, because he suddenly seemed cold and a little distant, if she had offended him. Then without even waiting to watch her climb the staircase, he bowed and walked away.

She went to bed to worry about his reaction. She lay in the darkness thinking over everything that had occurred since he had met them on *The Osaka*.

'He is so strangely unpredictable,' she told herself.

She remembered how everyone who knew him had told her how fantastic and splendid he was! What a showman! What an unusual personality! But no-one so far had suggested that he was far more cultured than any man she had ever met.

She could imagine her father, knowledgeable on English architecture, perhaps appreciating the Chinese pictures, but he would not understand them.

Most of all she could not imagine such things mattering to any of the gentlemen who came to Alderburne Park as they obviously mattered to Maximus Kirby.

What was he really like, this strange, unpredictable man who was soon to be her brother-in-law?

"My brother-in-law!"

Dorinda whispered the words into the darkness and turned her face against the pillow in a vain attempt to evade the pain of them.

Chapter Six

Dorinda wandered through the cool dimness of the big Sitting-Room to stand looking into the garden.

Fluttering over the orchids was a profusion of butterflies, each one more brilliant and colourful than the next, crimson, orange, yellow, vermilion, and turquoise. They had a grace which seemed somehow even more poignant than the flowers over which they hovered.

She had grown used to many things since she had been in Singapore, but the beauty of the butterflies never ceased to thrill her.

Dorinda stood seeing the sunshine, warm and golden, covering everything with a shimmering haze, and felt with a little throb in her heart that all too soon she would be back in the rain, sleet and cold of England.

Then her eczema would return and once again she would become a ghost-like creature moving about Alderburne Park afraid to meet anyone, determined not to be seen.

Her old jobs and household chores would be waiting for her. She could almost hear her father's voice saying:

"Where is Dorinda? Let her cope with it."

Or her mother's softer tones murmuring plaintively:

"Do arrange everything, Dorinda. I really cannot talk to Chef when he is in this sort of mood."

It would all be just as before and after a few weeks it would be as if she had never been away and she would have nothing but memories.

Memories of the butterflies; of the sunshine; of looking pretty; talking; laughing and at her ease when meeting people. Above all, memories of Maximus Kirby!

This was her sixth day in his house, and yet, incredible though it seemed, since the first night when he had shown her his treasures they had never had a conversation alone together.

She had begun to learn as the days passed how much work he did and how incessantly busy it kept him.

There were always people to luncheon and to dinner—notabilities passing through the Port, Chinese Mandarins in their long robes, traders affecting Western dress but appearing unmistakably Chinese whatever they wore.

There were officials from the East India Company, Captains and Officers from battle-ships of all countries, Residents and Colonial Secretaries from every part of Malaya and surrounding islands.

It did not seem possible that any man could have such a variety of interests or could pack so much into the hours of each day.

Maximus Kirby rose very early and long before his guests were stirring, he was downstairs either in his office or else out riding on a spirited horse which Dorinda learnt was the way he preferred to get his exercise.

Yet even though he rose early and went to bed late, there was so much that required his attention, his judgment, his authority, that sometimes listening to him at the dining-table Dorinda wondered if any other man could have as much energy or enthusiasm for what he was doing.

"Mr. Kirby is amazing!" she said to Lee Chang Lo.

This was Maximus Kirby's private secretary, a very clever Chinaman who, Dorinda learnt, had been with him since he first came to Singapore.

He held all the strings of his employer's personal Empire in his long-nailed fingers.

"A lot of it is organisation, Miss Hyde," Lee Chang Lo replied in perfect English.

Dorinda looked curious and he continued:

"Only Mr. Kirby is sensible enough not to waste time in waiting for conveyances; for people to pack for him; or for a ship to sail."

"What do you mean by that?"

"There are always carriages outside the front door both day and night," Lee Chang Lo replied. "If Mr. Kirby wishes to go out, they are there waiting. He does not have to send to the stables."

"I can see that is sensible!" Dorinda exclaimed.

"Both Mr. Kirby's yachts are always ready to put to sea the moment he steps on board," Lee Chang Lo went on.

"Both yachts?"

"Mr. Kirby has a Steam-Yacht, *The Sea Dragon*, on which you arrived, and another *The Sea Nymph*, a sailing yacht, which you must ask him to show you. It is a huge Chinese junk which he captured from a pirate, and had it fitted out with every comfort."

"It sounds fascinating."

"On board each yacht Mr. Kirby keeps a double set of clothes," Lee Chang Lo explained, "so that if he decides to go anywhere in the world when he is down in the town, there is no delay."

Dorinda clapped her hands together.

"You are right! It is very clever!" she said. "I do see that there is not a moment wasted on mundane things. It gives Mr. Kirby more time for what is important, and I am sure that in particular you are very essential to him."

The Chinese bowed and then, as if Dorinda had reminded him of his duty, left her alone.

It was the thoughtfulness that Maximus Kirby showed over small details which surprised her most.

She could understand a man in his position being careful where business was concerned not to let anything escape his notice, but his generosity to Letty was only exceeded by the manner in which every present he gave her had a meaning.

The second day after their arrival she received, besides the necklace and bracelet to match her engagement ring, a brooch in the shape of a Bird of Paradise, its breast and plumage all of coloured gems.

It was beautiful, and both Dorinda and Sister Teresa were fascinated by the workmanship which had created it.

But Letty was not interested in it for long, any more than she seemed to care for the necklace which Maximus Kirby gave her a day or two later, comprised of enamelled butterflies, their ruby and diamond bodies linked together by emeralds.

Dorinda could understand his thoughtfulness for Letty, but she was very touched when she too received presents, although they were very different.

First, as she half anticipated, she received, at the same time that Letty was given her Bird of Paradise brooch, a piece of jade.

She felt embarrassed as she opened the little Chinese box in which it was enclosed, knowing that she had almost asked for it and yet there was nothing she could do but accept it graciously.

It was apple-green, in the shape of a small Chinese dragon.

She looked it up in the books which she had brought for the journey from England, and was certain that it belonged to the Ching Dynasty.

It was later than some of the pieces owned by Maximus Kirby, but at the same time exquisitely carved and of a brighter green.

The next day she received a Chinese ivory.

It was so intricately carved that it was hard to believe it had been done by human hands.

"Look at the detail!" Dorinda exclaimed.

"The Chinese are masters of detail," Sister Teresa replied. "I remember a lady who tore her Paris gown. Although it was neatly darned, she would not wear it and decided to have the whole dress copied by a Chinese tailor."

She laughed.

"He copied it exactly, including the darn!"

The ivory was housed in a little wooden box made of embroidery with a silk lining.

"I think a present," Dorinda said to Sister Teresa, "is even more fascinating when it is beautifully packed."

"The Chinese excel at making these boxes," Sister Teresa said, "but to them every present is a ceremonial gift, something which is long remembered."

"I will always remember my gifts," Dorinda said and tried to think how they would look in her bed-room at Alderburne Park.

Every day she stroked her little jade dragon so that it would keep away evil thoughts, and she knew as she did so that the evil she was conscious of was jealousy!

It was hard not to be jealous of Letty, not because of her jewellery or the comfort and wealth she would know as Maximus Kirby's wife, but because she could be with him.

Could anything be more fascinating, Dorinda asked herself, than listening to a man who could speak on so many varied subjects? Who knew so much, who had hidden, undiscovered depths to his character of which few people were aware?

She knew, despite every resolution to the contrary that she was glad that Maximus Kirby had not taken Letty into the rooms where he kept his very special treasures.

He had taken her round the new house as he had taken Dorinda, and Letty had said the right things about the ornaments, pictures and the huge Chinese porcelain dragons which Maximus Kirby told her guarded the house from demons.

"There are other guards also," he said quickly when he saw the look of apprehension in her eyes, "and they are on duty day and night. So you need not be afraid! Not that I think that anyone in Singapore would attempt to rob me!"

At the insistence of Sister Teresa Letty made an effort to appear at meals, but usually by the evening she was tired, and out of the six evenings they had been in Singapore, she had been down to dinner only twice.

Dorinda tried to tell her afterwards about the guests and how interesting they were, but Letty would not listen.

"Too many people!" she said positively, "and they talk too much, it makes my head ache."

"But, Letty, you will have to be Hostess to them," Dorinda insisted in dismay.

"No!" Letty said firmly.

For the last two days she had not complained so much or reiterated so often that she wished to go home. She had a new interest in the Chinese children whom Sister Teresa had taken her to see at the Mission-School.

Dorinda had gone with them and had quite understood how fascinating the little Chinese were—the boys with their long pig-tails and the girls with their dark hair piled on top of their tiny heads.

Their small round faces and slanting eyes made them look, as Letty said, "like little dolls." It was with the greatest difficulty that Sister Teresa could persuade her to leave the Mission.

She talked of nothing else and even the present of a pearl necklace from Maximus Kirby did not divert her attention.

"They are very valuable and very beautiful pearls," Sister Teresa said to Dorinda.

As she spoke, Dorinda could not help remembering what the Doctor and the Purser had said about Maximus Kirby's mistress, "Perfect Pearl," to whom he had given so many strings that they wondered how her slim neck could carry them all.

It was easy to visualise how alluring "Perfect Pearl" had been, and why Maximus Kirby had been fascinated by her.

He could have any woman he liked in this Kingdom of his, Dorinda thought to herself, and wondered why in the circumstances he wished to be married.

The next day she was sitting at luncheon next to Sir Hugh Lowe, the Resident of Perak, who she had learnt had been instrumental in bringing a new prosperity to the State.

When he had arrived in office, Perak was burdened by a heavy debt with no visible resources to meet it.

Sir Hugh's cleverness, with the help of Maximus Kirby, in promoting trade was beginning to swing the revenue the other way.

"I cannot tell you," he said to Dorinda, "how wonderfully Mr. Kirby has helped me with all my schemes and with my plans for the future."

"He seems to help everyone," Dorinda replied. "I cannot understand why he has not been made Governor of Singapore."

Sir Hugh Lowe smiled.

"We are doing our best to get rid of the present Governor."

"Why?"

"He was appointed two years ago," Sir Hugh answered, "and he has not yet even visited Malaya!"

"He has never been here?" Dorinda exclaimed, "but how extraordinary! No wonder someone else has to do all the work!"

"Mr. Kirby and I have been pulling every string possible, and I think we have succeeded, to get Sir Frederick Weld appointed. He has been Governor of Western Australia and Tasmania and should be of great service to Singapore."

"But why not Mr. Kirby?" Dorinda questioned.

"He is still very young," Sir Hugh answered. "He is also at present un-married, though this disadvantage is to be rectified."

"You mean that then there would be a chance of his receiving the Appointment?"

"Sir Frederick has made it clear that he cannot stay many years. He is too old, for one thing, and when he retires I think there will be no question as to who will take his place."

'Now I understand,' Dorinda thought to herself, 'why Maximus Kirby wishes to be married!'

It was obvious, seeing the amount of entertaining required by him, that he must have a Hostess.

Also, as a Governor was usually Knighted either

before or soon after he took Office, the Queen would
appoint only a person of unblemished reputation and
who lived, at least officially, a blameless and respectable
life!

"Perfect Pearl" and "Goldie" would certainly not be
appropriate for the personal representative of her Britannic Majesty, Empress of India. Therefore Maximus
Kirby had decided that he would be married!

Now that Dorinda had the key as to why he had
made the decision, she could understand exactly what
had happened.

Maximus Kirby had gone to England in search of
machinery, contractors, horses and a wife.

He had met her father at the Club. Perhaps in telling
him of the Earl's excellent horse-flesh, someone had also
mentioned the beauty of his daughter.

It had all happened so smoothly and so easily. He
had come to Alderburne Park and one look at Letty
could have convinced him that this was exactly the wife
that he required as Governor of Singapore.

Not only was she beautiful, which to him would be
essential, but Letty also had breeding and background
to enhance her desirability.

There had been no obstacles to his suit and Letty
had come out to marry him.

Now that Maximus Kirby had met her without the
restrictive presence of her father and mother, what did
he feel?

The question was too frightening for Dorinda to find
an answer. But because she now understood how important Maximus Kirby's marriage was to his plans for
the future, she redoubled her efforts to make Letty
understand what was expected of her.

Somtimes Letty listened when Dorinda talked to her,
but more often than not she sat with a vacant expression
on her face, obviously hearing very little of what was
said and paying no attention.

This morning when Dorinda went in to see her she
was petulant.

"Go away, Dorinda!" she cried. "I do not want to

hear what you have to say. I want to be with Sister Teresa and I want to go and see the little Chinese children."

"You cannot do that this morning."

"Why not?" Letty asked, immediately beginning to pout at the thought of not getting what she wanted.

"Because we are having an early luncheon," Dorinda said, "and we are going out to see Mr. Kirby's plantations. You know he told you about them, and you promised you would like to see them."

Letty shrugged her shoulders.

"It is important, Letty," Dorinda insisted. "The experiments he is making may make a great deal of difference to the prosperity of Singapore."

"I do not want to see plantations!"

"They are very interesting," Dorinda cajoled, "and there will be lots of Chinese and Malayan children working with their fathers and mothers."

"It is too hot!"

"We are not leaving until it is cooler. You will have time for a siesta after luncheon. You can sleep, Letty, and then you will feel bright and you will enjoy the drive. I believe it is very beautiful."

Letty seemed inclined to argue, so Dorinda left the room knowing that an argument might send her into a tantrum. It was far better to let her adjust herself to the idea, so that there would be no surprise when the time came for them to leave.

Dorinda went downstairs.

She knew Maximus Kirby had meetings that morning in the town and the house was very quiet.

On an impulse she walked down the passages towards the old house. She had never been there since the first evening Mr. Kirby had taken her there.

She had hoped he might suggest that she should visit the rooms again to look at the porcelain and the pictures, but he had not mentioned it and she had the feeling that perhaps he regretted showing her anything so intimate.

'Perhaps I only imagined the place was different

from the rest of the house,' Dorinda said to herself now.

With a determination that was in some way unusual she walked towards the court-yard which was even lovelier than she remembered.

She had learnt that it was called "The Court-Yard of Soft Words."

She thought perhaps that in the past when the house was first built the wives, and perhaps the concubines of the owner, had sat there and talked softly to each other in their musical voices.

The door into the room with the jade was open. Dorinda looked around at the centuries-old treasures which Maximus Kirby had collected.

She noticed a carving of a flowering lotus in white and pale green nephrite. It was so delicately executed that one could almost see the petals opening.

There was a Chinese goddess in coral and a disc ornamented with dragons which Dorinda had noticed before. She thought it must have been carved hundreds of years B.C.

She lingered for a while amongst the jade, and then because it drew her with invisible hands she passed through the embroidered hanging into the further room.

Instantly she was struck again with the feeling of peacefulness, and she was as sure as she had been before that it was here that Maximus Kirby came when the problems he had to solve seemed too overwhelming, or the difficulties insurmountable.

It was just as if one received a cool hand on a feverish forehead, and now Dorinda looked first as she had done before at the little Täng horse and then at some of the other pottery, before her eyes rose to the pictures.

She was sure that she had not been mistaken in her interpretation of the first one. The great barren crag was a vivid contrast to the flowers and the still pool beneath it.

She turned to the other picture to look again at the flowing stream with the clouds above it, and above them the high mountain peaks.

She noticed now, as she had not done so before, that prior to reaching the bridge the stream was divided. It was shown by only a few strokes of the brush, but she knew that the artist had meant to portray that two streams were joined by the bridge and became one.

Dorinda stood looking at the picture for a long time. Various interpretations came to her mind and yet she was not sure which was the right one.

Finally with a litle sigh she went from the room, feeling almost as if she had been in a Church and that she had been sustained and helped by something beyond herself.

It was getting near to luncheon time as she went up the stairs to Letty's room.

To her surprise neither Sister Teresa nor Letty was there!

They did not in fact arrive back until after luncheon was ready and Maximus Kirby was waiting.

There were several guests, but if he was annoyed at Letty being late he did not show it. He greeted her with a smile and as usual raised her hand to his lips.

"I must apologise," Sister Teresa said. "I have broken my watch and I did not realise how late it was."

"I see I shall have to give you another one," Maximus Kirby replied.

"It will be much more economical to get the one I already have repaired," Sister Teresa said.

"We might do that as well," he answered. "It is always wise to have something in reserve."

"That is exactly like you, Kirby!" one of the guests exclaimed. "You always have something in reserve. That is why you are so successful!"

They were all laughing at this as they went into the Dining-Room.

Letty was looking extremely lovely in a pale blue gown which echoed the blue of her eyes.

She was in one of her better moods and apparently not tired by what she and Sister Teresa had been doing that morning.

It was however important that she should have a

rest, and Dorinda hurried her away as soon as luncheon was finished so that she could lie down on her bed.

The room was quite cool, as there were two punkahs moving in it, and it was scented by several vases of flowers. There was also the fragrance of the blossoms coming through the window from the garden.

"Try to sleep, Letty," Dorinda urged. "I want you to enjoy seeing all that Mr. Kirby is going to show us this afternoon."

"You will be coming?" Letty asked.

"Yes, if you want me," Dorinda answered. "But it would be nicer if you and Mr. Kirby went alone."

"I want you to come with us," Letty said obstinately.

"Then I will," Dorinda promised.

She knew that she would have been very disappointed if she had been left behind, but at the same time she would have been so willing to do so if Letty had wished it.

It had been arranged that Sister Teresa should go into the town in the afternoon to attend to the many personal matters for which Letty's claims had left her no time.

"I will help you get her dressed," Sister Teresa said to Dorinda, "and then I will slip off and put my own affairs in order. I really ought to leave for Sarawak before the wedding."

"Oh, please, you must not do that!" Dorinda cried in alarm. "I cannot imagine how Letty is going to do without you as it is, and I have not begun to tell her yet what the ceremony is to be like."

Sister Teresa looked at Dorinda with a little smile in her eyes.

They both knew that Maximus Kirby was thinking up new spectacular features for his magnificent marriage day after day.

There were now to be so many entertainments and amusements at the Reception that the whole thing would be almost like a Fair.

Dorinda might in fact have thought the whole thing

rather vulgar if she had not known that it was what the Chinese expected.

To them marriage was a very important event. It started with the preliminaries being arranged by a professional Bride-seeker or Matrimonial Agent. Then an Astrologer would be consulted to know if the union between the two persons chosen was likely to prove propitious.

If his verdict was favourable, presents were exchanged; the man sending a gold ring and jewels to his future bride; the girl sending in return a gold hairpin or a jewel. They were then betrothed.

According to Lee Chang Lo whom Dorinda had questioned, a Chinese bridegroom seldom or even never saw his betrothed until the wedding-day.

For that day there were innumerable preparations, all of which had a special significance.

Candles, paper dragons, trays of fish, fruit, silk and cotton sarongs, two ducks, a roast pig, a roast goat, and dozens of other items were exchanged between the bridal pair.

After the ceremony a procession conducted the bride to the bridegroom's house and a great number of crackers and fireworks were fired off for good luck.

"Three days after the marriage," Lee Chang Lo had said, "all the friends of the newly married couple send money and presents to them. On the expiration of twelve days, the bride's parents give a feast at which the newly married couple are of course the guests of honour.

"Is that the end?" Dorinda enquired.

"No! Not until the end of the month, when the bride pays her parents a formal visit, are the ceremonies completed."

"It sounds very complicated!" Dorinda exclaimed. "Does this happen at every wedding when a Chinaman marries?"

"He may have three or four wives," Lee Chang Lo replied, "but as a rule, here in the Straits, a Chinaman has only one wife. If he takes other women to his house they are treated as concubines. But the children of all the wives are on an equal footing and no difference is made between them."

"What happens when the father dies?"

"He leaves his wealth to be divided equally among all his male offspring," Lee Chang Lo answered.

It was obvious that if a poor Chinaman would take such trouble over his wedding, he would expect Maximus Kirby to multiply everything he could do a million times.

To Dorinda it was all very understandable, but she knew it was not going to be easy to make Letty accept such festivities and to take part in them willingly.

She had learnt there was to be an enormous display of fireworks as soon as it grew dark and she knew she would have to ask about this.

It was an inevitable finale to any wedding in the East, but Letty loathed fireworks, and the noise would obviously remind her of the pirates.

There was, Dorinda thought, the chance that the bride and bridegroom would have left on their honeymoon before the fireworks were let off. If not, she would have to speak to Maximus Kirby about it.

But how difficult it was to know what to say!

Dorinda went to her own room and read.

She seldom slept after luncheon. It seemed such a waste of time.

'There will be plenty of time to sleep on the voyage home,' she told herself dismally.

Instead she read books she had found in a very comprehensive Library that Maximus Kirby had built into the new part of the house.

If she had not already known how wide his interests were, she would have been aware of it from the books he had chosen.

They ranged from Histories of the East to Biographies from the West, Chinese books of great age, which unfortunately she could not understand, and novels in French which she was able to enjoy for the first time.

Her father had never wanted to "waste" money on

books and her grandfather's collection which she enjoyed was sadly out of date.

Dorinda read quickly, but she thought despairingly there would be no time to get through a hundredth of the books in Maximus Kirby's Library before she was forced to leave.

Now, although immersed in what she was reading, she kept an eye on the clock and then dressed herself early so as to have plenty of time for Letty.

She went along to her sister's room. Before she opened the door she heard voices and realised that Sister Teresa was arguing with Letty.

"You are not tired, dear," the Sister was saying. "If you get up, you will feel better."

"I do not want to get up," Letty replied, "not unless I can go to the Mission and play with the children."

"They will not be there this afternoon and you promised Mr. Kirby you would go and see his plantations."

"I am too tired," Letty said positively.

"Oh, Letty, you cannot disappoint him!" Dorinda interposed. "He is so looking forward to showing you his crops. He has been talking about them for several days and I have explained to you how interesting they are."

"I am not going!" Letty cried again.

She turned over as she spoke and shut her eyes.

The firm way she closed her lips told Dorinda she was in one of her really obstinate moods.

Dorinda and Sister Teresa pleaded, cajoled and besought her, but it was no use. She was determined not to go to the plantations.

In the end Dorinda reluctantly had to go downstairs and tell Maximus Kirby who was waiting for them that Letty was not well.

"I am afraid . . . the heat has been . . . too much for her," she said hesitatingly, not looking at him because she did not wish to see the disappointment in his eyes.

"I thought it was rather cooler," he said dryly.

"Perhaps it would have been better if Letty had not gone out this morning."

"She certainly seemed in good spirits at luncheon time," Maximus Kirby remarked. "Well, if she cannot manage it we shall have to leave it for another day."

Because she knew he was annoyed, Dorinda said hesitatingly:

"I might . . . not be . . . here another day. I . . . suppose you would not . . . take me?"

"Would you really like to go?"

"I would love it! But not if it is any trouble," Dorinda answered.

"I have left the afternoon free to go to the plantations," he said, "and as a matter of fact, there are several things I want to do there. So, if you are prepared to come with me . . ."

"Please take me," she begged with a sudden light in her eyes.

"Very well then, let us go."

"Give me two seconds to get my hat."

Maximus Kirby snapped his fingers and gave an order. A Chinese boy ran up the stairs to return with Dorinda's hat, sunshade and her reticule which she had left lying on a table in her room.

She put her hat on her head without even looking in a mirror and she hurried after Maximus Kirby down the front steps.

Under the portico in front of the door she saw not the Victoria she had expected they would ride in but a Phaeton which only seated two.

It was not one of the high, rather ridiculous Phaetons that were seen in London Parks, but a serviceable, lightly sprung vehicle drawn by two horses. It had large wheels which Dorinda knew added to its speed.

"It is considerably faster," Maximus Kirby explained, as if he knew what she was thinking.

They set off moving so quickly that Dorinda soon realised it would be impossible to hold up her sunshade, and she was glad that her straw hat had ribbons which tied under her chin.

It was a glorious afternoon and since their route was high up it was not overwhelmingly hot.

They moved northwards into the interior of the country along narrow flower-edged roads.

There were forests of trees, most of them in blossom, and the beauty was almost indescribable.

They had driven for over an hour before they came to the first of Maximus Kirby's plantations.

"I have been making experiments with all types of crops," he told Dorinda as they travelled, "tapioca, sweet potatoes, sago, tobacco, sugar-cane and pineapple. But now in the last nine years we have been developing something new in Malaya, something which I believe will make an enormous difference to the economy of the country."

"What is that?" Dorinda asked.

"Rubber!" he answered.

"I thought rubber already came from this part of the world."

"Not yet," he answered. "The rubber you have in Europe was discovered by the Spaniards in South America."

"Yes, of course. I remember that now."

"One of their Priests described an Aztec game played with balls 'made of the juice of a certain herbe, which being stricken upon the ground, but softly rebounded incredibly into the eyer'."

Dorinda laughed.

"It has certainly been useful for other things since!"

"One of the most useful, although I cannot imagine you in one, is of course a mackintosh," Maximus Kirby remarked.

"I have read about that," Dorinda said, pleased she could show her knowledge. "The man who discovered how it could be manufactured was a Scottish chemist called Charles Macintosh."

"You are very knowledgeable, Miss Hyde," Maximus Kirby remarked. "Perhaps we read the same books! Anyhow it convinced me that it could be of great importance for Malaya to grow rubber trees, and they were brought here by Sir Charles Markham, a brilliant man."

"I have heard of him," Dorinda murmured.

"He has carried out experiments at the Botanical Gardens at Kew, which have convinced him that rubber can be grown in India and Malaya, and now you will see my rubber plantation and how the trees are developing."

"I do hope your experiment succeeds!" Dorinda exclaimed.

As she spoke she was certain he would be successful. She felt that though he might challenge fate with all his ideas, he would inevitably be the victor.

'Fate must be a woman!' Dorinda thought whimsically.

At any rate she was sure every woman except Letty would find Maximus Kirby irresistible. She dared not express even to herself what she felt at being beside him and alone!

There were however other plantations to inspect first.

Everywhere there were buffaloes, heavy and ponderous, making strange noises as they moved and looking almost like pre-historic beasts.

They rose out of the swamps and plodded, dripping wet, over the dry fields, often driven by tiny Malayan children who ordered them about with a tone of authority.

"The Indian farmers prefer cows, and the Chinese keep ducks and pigs," Maximus Kirby remarked.

There were flocks of white ducks swimming wherever there was water.

'Meals for the thousands of Chinese in Singapore!' Dorinda thought.

They stopped at a plantation and the Overseer hurried to the Phaeton, eager to give Mr. Kirby a report on his progress.

Numbers of men and women were working side by side, their large, conical-shaped hats protecting them from the sun.

The ground looked fertile and all the crops seemed to be doing well.

Dorinda would have liked to talk to the coolies, but

she knew they would not understand her. Only the Overseers spoke English.

The plantations were bigger and the distance between them longer than she had expected.

She could not help realising that, since she and not Letty was accompanying him, Maximus Kirby was doing more business than he would have done had he been forced to worry about over-tiring his future wife.

"And now for my rubber plantation," he said with a touch of excitement in his voice.

They drove on and now Dorinda saw that he had cleared part of the virgin jungle to plant his new trees.

"You must not be disappointed," he said to her, "that the trees are not larger. We have not had much time for growth, and I do not suppose you realise that a rubber tree of the species we are using can sometimes grow to a height of a hundred and twenty feet and have a trunk girth of more than eighteen inches."

"It sounds enormous!" Dorinda remarked.

"It is!" he answered. "But the average is about sixty or eighty feet, and I shall be quite content with that!"

"When can you start tapping them . . . if that is the right word?" Dorinda enquired.

"Yes, tapping is correct, but it cannot be done until the tree is five or six years old. Then the rubber, or latex as it is called, is collected in a cup."

The trees were well spaced and Maximus Kirby explained it was usual, as he had done, to protect them with an outer planting of coffee or cocoa bushes.

They drove slowly until he drew the horses to a standstill outside a small bungalow obviously newly built. It was surrounded by a garden and situated at what appeared to Dorinda to be the very end of the plantation.

As if he read her thoughts Maximus Kirby said:

"This is only the beginning. In a month I am going to start to clear another great area of the jungle. That is why the bungalow is here. I plan it to be in the centre of the plantation."

An old Chinese man, too old to work, appeared. He

held the horses as they alighted, and then led them into the shade of some large trees.

Maximus Kirby assisted Dorinda from the Phaeton and asked in Chinese where the Overseer was. The old man pointed to where not far away Dorinda could now see through the low trees and bushes a man wearing a white shirt and trousers.

They walked towards him and Dorinda realised that this was the first English Overseer she had encountered on Maximus Kirby's land.

He was introduced to her as a Mr. Langton.

He was a pleasant-faced young man of perhaps twenty-seven and he greeted his employer with delight.

"How nice to see you, Mr. Kirby!" he exclaimed. "I was hoping you would pay me a visit. There are a great many things I would like to discuss with you."

"I had hoped to get here last week," Maximus answered, "but I could not manage it. What is the trouble?"

The Overseer was carrying a gun under his arm and now he laid it carefully against the trunk of a tree before he pulled some papers from his pocket.

"It is about this last shipment . . ." he began.

Dorinda, knowing that their business talk was not her concern, walked away.

She inspected the trees, noting the long, smooth green leaves which were about eighteen inches in length, and the yellowish-green blossoms which grew in clusters and in the distance looked very pretty.

She moved among them until she saw just ahead the high trees and the thick dark foliage of the jungle.

The trees were astonishing, their trunks enormously thick and some of them of an unbelievable height.

There were the lianas, twining themselves around the trunks, curving over the branches, joining tree to tree in an almost impenetrable mass.

Dorinda recognised the rattans of which she had read, which had long, tough, flexible stems and were able to climb because they had recurving thorns in the tips of their long leaves.

It was all fascinating and very beautiful, and she moved closer hoping she might see a large grotesque hornbill, a beautiful Argus-pheasant or even a highly-coloured trogon.

Despite what she had said to Letty, she realised these were birds that were seldom seen outside the jungle and were not to be found among the black and white magpie-robins, the sunbirds and kingfishers in Maximus Kirby's garden.

The scarlet-flowered lianas made vivid patches of colour against the dark foliage. The jungle seemed a strange, enchanted place, the haunt perhaps of dragons and witches!

Birds squalling as they flew from a tree high above made her start, and there was a sudden scuffle made by some small animal scuttling through the undergrowth.

She moved on anxious to see more, forgetting all prudence, conscious only of a feeling of adventure.

Then between the trunks of two great trees, half-obscured by the lianas and yet perfectly recognisable, she saw glaring at her two shining green eyes in a striped yellow fur.

It was a tiger!

Chapter Seven

Dorinda was paralysed into immobility.

She stood staring at the great beast, her eyes fixed on his. Somewhere vaguely at the back of her mind, she remembered hearing that if one kept absolutely still and motionless, an animal did not attack.

Then a low growl came from the tiger's throat. He opened his mouth to snarl, showing his teeth and she knew by the sudden tension of his neck and back that he was about to spring.

Yet she was frightened to the point where she could not run or do anything but stand helplessly waiting for his claws to tear her to pieces.

Suddenly there was an explosion in her ear and the whole forest seemed to vibrate with it.

The tiger fell with a thud amongst the undergrowth in which it had been standing and hundreds of birds rose from the trees with a noise that seemed as loud as the report from the gun.

Dorinda's ears were ringing and for a moment she could hardly believe that the danger had passed; that the animal would not spring on her.

Then she heard Maximus Kirby's voice furious with anger as he exclaimed:

"You little fool! What the hell do you mean by coming in here?"

With what was to her a superhuman effort, she turned her face towards him. He was standing just behind her and the fury on his face seemed to transform him.

He had saved her!

She wanted to put out her hands towards him and hide her face against his shoulder.

But before she could move or speak, Mr. Langton came running through the trees to join them.

"You've killed him!" he exclaimed. "Well done, Sir! I've been trying to get that tiger for the last ten days. He carried off one of the children on the Estate only a week ago."

Still with an expression of anger on his face Maximus Kirby handed Mr. Langton the gun.

"Take this!" he said. "I will help Miss Hyde back to the bungalow."

He put his hand as he spoke under Dorinda's elbow and led her back the way she had come through the trees and out into the open plantation.

She knew he was still extremely angry, and now the shock of what she had been through made her feel weak and curiously near to tears.

"I cannot imagine how you could have been so fool-hardy," Maximus Kirby said in the tone of a Nanny scolding a naughty child. "Surely you must have enough sense to know it is dangerous to go into the jungle unaccompanied?"

Dorinda wanted to reply but there was a constriction in her throat and she could not speak.

"Why did you go?" he went on as if he would force an answer from her. "What were you looking for?"

She felt she had to reply and knew how childish it would sound to say that it had seemed an enchanted forest.

Instead she said, her voice low and hesitating:

"I . . . I was looking . . . at the . . . trees and . . . the flowers."

They had by now reached the steps to the verandah which surrounded the bungalow and Maximus Kirby released her arm.

Then, as he looked at the pallor of her face in which her eyes, wide and still frightened, looked very large, he said, in a different tone which held a hint of laughter in it:

"If you wanted flowers, what is wrong with these?"

He bent down as he spoke and picked one of the wild orchids which were growing at the foot of the steps. There were half-a-dozen pink blossoms clustered on one stem.

As he did so there was a hiss and something black and swift lashed out at him.

It happened so quickly that Dorinda knew that if she had not been watching what he was doing she would not have realised what occurred nor noticed the variegated black body slither away.

She gave a little cry! Maximus Kirby without a word pulled off his coat and dragged back the cuff of his shirt.

There on the outside of his arm some inches above the wrist on his sun-burnt skin were two small punctures.

As he stared at them Dorinda acted.

She seized his arm, her fingers right above the marks so as to force the blood down and then her mouth was against his skin sucking with all her strength.

She heard him give an exclamation, but he did not take his arm away and now Mr. Langton came running up.

"What has happened?" he asked.

"A viper!"

Mr. Langton put down the gun and pulled a handkerchief from his pocket. He tied it round Maximus Kirby's arm while Dorinda still sucked the punctures.

She felt the venom come into her mouth and when she could suck no more she spat it out.

"Wipe it from your tongue as well as your mouth," Maximus Kirby said sharply.

As he spoke he gave her his handkerchief with his free hand. It was of soft linen and smelt of Eau de Cologne.

Dorinda did as she was told, rubbing her tongue roughly in case any of the snake's venom remained on it.

Then she saw what Mr. Langton held in his hand.
It was a knife, gleaming silver in the sunlight.

"Cut deep!" Maximus Kirby said quietly.

Mr. Langton cut into the arm twice. Dorinda, her
eyes on Maximus Kirby's face, saw his lips tighten with
the pain, but he did not speak or move.

The blood poured down over his wrist in a red tide
and Mr. Langton's hands were stained with it. He
released the tourniquet and tied his handkerchief over
the wound.

"Whisky, Sir?" the young man said. "Will you walk
into the house?"

"Of course."

Maximus Kirby ascended the steps up to the verandah and Mr. Langton ran ahead to pull open the wire-
covered door which opened into the Sitting-Room.

It was a small room, sparsely furnished. On a side-
table stood a bottle of whisky and several glasses.

Mr. Langton picked up the bottle which was three-
quarters full and filled a tumbler to the brim.

He handed it without words to his employer who
drank it quickly.

"You must keep walking, Sir, in case there is a
chance of your going into a coma."

"I am well aware of that!" Maximus Kirby replied.

"I will send a boy for the Doctor. It may take some
time, but I will tell him to travel as quickly as possible."

Maximus Kirby did not answer. He finished the
whisky he held in his hand and refilled the glass.

For the first time since it happened Dorinda felt he
looked at her.

"I will try not to be unpleasantly drunk," he said
with what was almost a smile on his lips.

"It does not matter if you are," she said in a low
voice, "just start walking. You know that is the right
thing to do."

She remembered how her father had described to
her what had happened when one of his friends, one
very hot summer, had been bitten by an adder.

She had recalled that what had saved his life was the

fact that they had sucked the poison from his wound, made it bleed, filled him up with whisky and kept him walking up and down until the fever had broken and the danger had passed.

It must have been her memory of that which had prompted her to act so quickly when she realised it was a viper that had bitten Maximus Kirby.

The viper was of the same species as an adder, and she knew that she and Mr. Langton had done exactly what was required up to this moment.

Maximus Kirby drank down the second glass of whisky and began walking slowly but firmly across the room and back again.

It was only a short distance because the bungalow was small. Seeing another door, Dorinda opened it.

There as she had expected was the bed-room, and she saw it would be easy if she moved the table for Maximus Kirby to walk across the whole bungalow and back, traversing the two rooms.

She moved the table in the Sitting-Room and a chair in the bed-room. He understood what she was trying to do, and walked from one room to the other and back again.

Mr. Langton returned.

"I have sent a boy for the Doctor," he said. "He is a fast runner and he knows where Doctor Seng lives."

"How long do you think it will take him?" Dorinda asked.

"Perhaps two hours," Mr. Langton replied. "We are a long way from Singapore and it will be dark before he gets there."

He looked at Maximus Kirby and realising he was walking a little unsteadily said:

"Put your arm on my shoulder, Sir. It will be easier if I help you."

Afterwards Dorinda could never remember exactly when she realised that Maximus Kirby was sagging and she had gone to his other side.

She had to pull his arm around her shoulder and

when she touched his hand she found it was burning hot and knew he had a high fever.

This was what they feared, as the poison invaded the body.

Mr. Langton persuaded Maximus Kirby to drink what was left of the bottle of whisky. Then they moved up and down the room getting slower and slower as the hours passed and it became more and more difficult for Maximus Kirby to realise what he had to do.

It was only his tremendous will-power, Dorinda realised, that kept him going, that forced his fever-wracked body to do what was required of it.

He did not speak. No sound came from between his lips. After a while he closed his eyes and there was only the sound of their footsteps on the uncarpeted floor.

When night fell the old Chinaman came in with an oil-lamp which he set down on the table.

He said something to Mr. Langton.

"Wong says that he has unharnessed the horses and stabled them for the night."

"Please thank him," Dorinda said.

She wondered if it would have been better if she had attempted to drive the Phaeton back to Singapore in search of the Doctor. But even as she thought it, she doubted whether she could have controlled the spirited horses which Maximus Kirby handled so expertly, or find the way.

They had travelled along so many different tracks during the afternoon that she was not even certain in which direction Singapore lay, and besides she could not have arrived before it was dark.

There was nothing else they could do, other than what they had done already, she thought helplessly.

Then with a sudden fear because Maximus Kirby's arm was so heavy, she wondered if he would die.

At the thought of it a pain ran through her like the poison of the snake that she had sucked from his arm.

He could not die! It was impossible!

When they had spoken about it jokingly that first

night on the yacht she had told him there was so much for him to do.

'How could Singapore manage without him?' she thought. 'He is needed here.'

And yet she was afraid.

Now as they walked through the Sitting-Room, into the bed-room and back again, she began to pray.

'Please God, save him! Make him well. Do not let this harm him. He cannot die! He cannot!'

And as she prayed she faced frankly and for the first time how much she loved him.

She had loved him since she had seen him stepping out of her father's Phaeton at Alderburne Park. She had loved him as hidden behind the carved screen of the Minstrels' Gallery she listened to him talking. She had loved him when she had seen him step up the gang-way onto *The Osaka* with eyes only for Letty.

She was aware now that the emotion she had felt when she had watched him kissing Mrs. Thompson had been simple jealousy; that ever since they had arrived in his house, she had waited only for the moments when she could see him and hear his voice. It might have been from the other end of the table, but that had been enough!

It was as if time stood still in an indescribable emptiness except when he was present.

'I love you! I love you!' Dorinda told him wordlessly.

Then she prayed with a passionate intensity which came from the very depths of her being that he might live.

The hours passed and still they kept walking.

The sweat was pouring down Mr. Langton's face and Dorinda knew that his shirt was soaked. She could feel that her gown was wet through where Maximus Kirby's heavy arm rested.

She touched his hand and it was still burning hot. She looked up at his face and saw there was a strange pallor beneath the superficial sun-burn on his skin.

"Surely the Doctor should be here by now!" she exclaimed and her voice was frightened.

"He might be out on a call," Mr. Langton answered and his voice was hoarse and dry. "There is a Chinese Festival today. I let the coolies off early. They have all gone to the village, about a mile-and-a-half away."

"Is there nothing else we can do?" Dorinda asked desperately.

"Nothing," he answered, "except to keep him walking."

That was easier said than done. Dorinda was almost exhausted by the weight of Maximus Kirby's arm and she knew that Mr. Langton, even though he was young and strong, was feeling the burden of his employer.

Backwards and forwards—turn—walk forward—turn—walk back again.

They must have done it a thousand times.

'I cannot go on!' Dorinda thought to herself, but she knew she could not fail the man she loved.

He must live! He must!

Now she closed her eyes and moved automatically. Sometimes it seemed almost too much effort to drag her foot forward, or to brace her body to turn at the outside wall.

She felt Maximus Kirby's arm slipping from her shoulder. With an effort she reached up to pull it back into position and when she touched it, it was wet!

She could not believe it!

She put her hand over his, feeling the skin damp beneath her fingers.

Then as they reached the Sitting-Room and the light of the oil-lamp was on his face, she looked up at him.

There were beads of sweat on his forehead and running down his cheeks.

"The fever has broken!" she cried.

It should have been a cry of joy but her voice was only a tired croak.

"My God, so it has!" Mr. Langton exclaimed. "Let us get him on to the bed."

They dragged Maximus Kirby into the bed-room, and lowered him down on the narrow bed-stead, resting his head against the pillows, then lifting his feet onto the cover.

Mr. Langton brought the lamp from the Sitting-Room and Dorinda could see they were not mistaken.

The fever had broken! Now there was no pallor beneath the sun-burn and Maximus Kirby looked like a man ordinarily asleep!

Dorinda crossed to the wash-stand. There was a towel on the table beside a ewer of water.

She dipped the towel in the water and wringing it out went to the bed and gently wiped Maximus Kirby's face. Mr. Langton had removed his shoes and he lay breathing evenly.

"There is nothing more we can do now until the Doctor arrives," Mr. Langton said.

He walked unsteadily into the Sitting-Room and Dorinda heard him throw himself down into one of the armchairs.

He was exhausted and so was she!

She stood for a moment by the bed-side looking down at Maximus Kirby, her heart going out to him.

"Thank You, God . . . thank You," she whispered.

Then, although she was not quite certain how it happened, she was sinking slowly onto the floor. As her head reached the mat which stood beside the bed, she fell asleep . . .

Dorinda awoke with a start to hear voices talking in the other room.

She was still lying on the floor but someone had put a pillow beneath her head and she knew it must have been Mr. Langton.

She scrambled to her feet as she heard a man say in the precise English used by Chinamen:

"I had just returned to my house when I found your boy waiting for me. He told me Mr. Kirby has been bitten by a snake."

"He was bitten by a viper, Dr. Seng, but the fever has broken."

"That is good. Can I see him?"

Dorinda was on her feet smoothing her crumpled skirt when Mr. Langton brought Doctor Seng into the bedroom.

"This is Miss Hyde," Mr. Langton said, "who sucked the poison from the snake's bite as soon as it happened."

"It was the right thing to do," Doctor Seng approved.

He was an elderly Chinaman with tired eyes but Dorinda had the impression he was dependable and confident of his own ability.

He examined Maximus Kirby's arm, inspecting the cuts made by Mr. Langton's knife.

"The wound is clean," he remarked.

He listened to Maximus Kirby's heart, took his pulse and put his hand on his forehead.

"He will sleep for some time," Doctor Seng said. "He has not only to get over the snake-bite, but the amount of whisky he has undoubtedly consumed."

"That is surely the right treatment?" Mr. Langton asked.

Doctor Seng smiled.

"It is the British treatment," he replied. "The Chinese use Snake-root."

"Is it effective?" Dorinda enquired.

She remembered she had heard of a herb which the Chinese and Malayans kept always at hand when working in the jungle.

"We think so," Doctor Seng replied. "I will leave you some, Mr. Langton. Persuade Mr. Kirby to take it as soon as he awakens."

He took a small packet from his bag and placed it beside the bed.

"He is strong and very healthy," the Doctor said. "But he should rest and stay where he is for another night. If he seems to wish to drive back to Singapore this afternoon, then give him one of these. It will make him sleep again."

The Doctor placed a small pill box beside the Snake-root. Then he looked at Dorinda.

"And you, Miss Hyde? You are all right?"

"Just a little tired, Doctor," Dorinda answered, "but

I am very happy to think that Mr. Kirby is out of danger."

Doctor Seng nodded his head.

"It was certainly your prompt action in sucking the wound which saved him," he said. "We have many non-venomous snakes in this part of the world, but the bite of the viper and the cobra can often be fatal!"

He picked up his bag.

"Are you returning to Singapore?" Dorinda asked.

"I am," the Doctor replied. "I have a number of patients waiting for me."

"Would it be too much to ask that I might accompany you? My sister and Sister Teresa are staying at Mr. Kirby's house and they will be very worried, I am sure, that we did not return last night."

"I shall be delighted, Miss Hyde, to convey you to them."

Mr. Langton insisted on Dorinda having a cup of tea before she left and the Doctor also accepted some refreshment.

Then they set off, driving in a small cart drawn by one ancient pony. It was very much slower and much more uncomfortable than when Dorinda had travelled behind Maximus Kirby's fine horse-flesh.

She could however hold her sun-shade over her head and, although the journey took a long time, she found it very interesting to talk with Doctor Seng.

He told her about the countryside, the customs and habits of the Chinese; the way Mr. Kirby had improved the conditions in which they worked and brought prosperity to so many homes in Singapore.

When they arrived at the house Dorinda thanked the Doctor and invited him in.

"I regret, Miss Hyde, I have no time to accept your most gracious hospitality," he said formally. "But may I say it has been a great pleasure to be in your auspicious company?"

Dorinda returned his formality and then she ran into the house to find Sister Teresa and Letty.

Knowing that they must have been much worried by

her absence, she half-expected to find them waiting in the Centre-Room. But they were not there and she started up the stairs to Letty's bed-room.

"Where is Lady Lettice?" she asked one of the Chinese servants on duty in the Hall.

"Ladies gone!" he replied.

'They must be visiting the Mission,' Dorinda thought to herself as she went on up the stairs.

She was surprised that they had not been more perturbed. Then she remembered that Sister Teresa would have been sure that she would be safe with Maximus Kirby.

And yet how easily she might have been dead! Mauled by the tiger!

Maximus Kirby too, could have lost his life because he bent to pick her a flower!

She reached the top of the stairs and knowing that Letty and Sister Teresa were out, she did not go towards Letty's bed-room but to her own.

It seemed very luxurious and beautiful after the austerity of Mr. Langton's bungalow.

She put down her sun-shade and took off her hat, throwing it onto a chair and walked across the room towards the window.

She never grew tired of looking out at the garden filled with flowers and blossom-laden trees.

Then she saw two letters lying on her dressing-table.

She thought quickly they must be from home, but at a second glance she saw that neither of them bore a stamp but were just addressed to her—one inscribed "Dorinda" and the other "Miss Hyde."

She had a strange feeling that there was something momentous about their lying there and quickly she picked up the one with only her Christian name, written in Letty's round, childish hand.

She opened the envelope, took a swift glance at the piece of paper inside and thought at first that through exhaustion she must have misread it. She read it again.

"Dearest Dorinda,

I am going away with Sister Teresa. I shall be very happy with her and I do not want to marry Mr. Kirby. Please tell him so. I am sorry if it makes Papa cross.

Love,
Letty."

Dorinda read it through twice and then with fingers which trembled she opened Sister Teresa's letter.

"Dear Lady Dorinda,

Letty has told me your real identity but I shall of course mention it to no-one. It is right that you, her sister, should understand that as a trained nurse I do not consider her capable of being married to any man, least of all to Mr. Maximus Kirby.

So I am taking her to Sarawak. I will look after Letty and I am sure she will be happy in the Mission, playing with the children.

I am doing this not only for her sake but for the man who has done so much for Singapore. I have for Mr. Maximus Kirby a great admiration and much gratitude. His career and his personal life must not be ruined by marrying a girl who could never by any possibility become the wife he requires. I leave it to you to explain to him why I have taken this step.

May God bless you,

Yours faithfully
in the love of Christ Jesus,
Sister Teresa

As Dorinda finished the letter she drew in a deep breath and sat down as if her legs could no longer support her.

She could not fully understand what had happened.

She felt as if her head was stuffed with cotton-wool, her mouth was dry and her lids were so heavy they felt like stones.

'There is nothing I can do about it,' she told herself.

Then because it seemed too difficult and too overwhelming a situation even to contemplate, she undressed and got into bed.

She slept all through the afternoon and awoke only when the sun was sinking, to lie trying to remember all that had happened.

It all came flooding back to her.

The tiger from which she had been saved by Maximus Kirby; the viper biting his arm; that terrible, exhausting walk backwards and forwards when he seemed likely to die.

And yet, while she had helped to support him, she had loved him unbearably!

Then the letters she had found on her return seemed to dance in front of her eyes.

'How could Letty and Sister Teresa have gone away and left me the impossible task of telling Maximus Kirby?' she asked herself.

He might not love Letty. She was quite certain it was impossible for her to have touched his heart. But he had chosen her as his wife. He had proclaimed their engagement even before she arrived in Singapore, and everyone who had come to the house had congratulated them both.

He had also planned his marriage.

"The Magnificent Marriage," which was to remain a vivid memory for all those who attended it!

Could anything be more humiliating, Dorinda thought, than that his bride should leave him a week before his wedding, because she preferred to be with Chinese children in a remote Catholic Mission than be his wife?

'It might have been better,' she told herself, 'if Letty had run away with another man!'

That would have been enough to hurt any man's pride, but to prefer a primitive native island to the security of being Mrs. Maximus Kirby was something it would be very hard to explain.

'How can I tell him?' she asked.

Because Dorinda felt so weak she forced herself to send for food and eat at least a few mouthfuls of the delicious dishes that were brought to her bed-side.

When the tray had been taken away she had lain staring into the darkness, feeling as if Letty's and Sister Teresa's letters were whirling round and round in her mind, repeating themselves over and over again.

She wondered now how it could ever have seemed possible to her father and to herself that Letty should marry a man like Maximus Kirby.

Yet at home at Alderburne Park, Letty had not seemed so abnormal as she did in different surroundings. First there had been her hysterics on being wrenched away from all that was familiar, then her physical fear of the storm in the Bay of Biscay, and finally the shock of the battle with the pirates.

No-one could have been kinder or more understanding than Maximus Kirby since she arrived.

Another man might have insisted on closer intimacies with his future wife. Or at least he might have demanded to be alone with her so that they could talk together without being eternally chaperoned either by Sister Teresa or Dorinda.

Maximus Kirby had not complained. He appeared to understand that Letty had suffered a severe shock from the noise of the battle and the fear that she might be murdered in her bed.

Still, he must have known! He must have realised from the very first, Dorinda told herself, that, beautiful though she was, Letty was not as other girls.

For one thing her preoccupation with the birds must have surprised him, and then her inability to take part in a conversation with any of the men who came to the house.

There were men who were of great importance in Maximus Kirby's life, who must have somehow without words conveyed the impression that whilst they admired Letty's exquisite loveliness, they found it impossible to talk to her.

At the same time Maximus Kirby meant to marry her, Dorinda told herself. He had made a bargain with her father and paid ten thousand pounds for the privilege of becoming the Earl's son-in-law.

It was like defaulting on a debt of honour that Letty should run away so casually and that Sister Teresa should have aided and abetted her.

At least Sister Teresa had been honest. She made it clear that she was doing this not only for Letty's sake but also for Maximus Kirby's.

There was no doubt that she loved him deeply in her own way and although it seemed strange to think of it, perhaps he brought out all that was maternal in her.

She was old enough to have been his mother and it is possible that spiritually, she thought of him as the son she could never have because of her vows of chastity.

Dorinda asked herself a question. If she had a son, would she want him to marry someone like Letty? She knew the answer was no.

"I want Mr. Kirby to be happy," she whispered into the darkness. "I cannot bear to think of him being hurt, disappointed or humiliated. He will be deeply disturbed by the people of Singapore laughing at him behind his back."

She drew in a deep breath.

"The Chinese will pity him because to them a promise of marriage is sacred. And men like Doctor Johnson and the Purser will talk and gossip and speculate about what has happened. And because Maximus Kirby is so intelligent, he will know exactly what they are saying."

Like a cry from the heart she said aloud:

"How can I help him? What can I do to make it better?"

She thought wildly that perhaps if she went down to the Quay she could board *The Sea Dragon* and sail after the ship on which Sister Teresa and Letty had embarked.

Maximus Kirby's fast yacht should be able to over-

take them, and she would try to persuade them to
return to Singapore! Even if they had reached Sarawak,
she might force Letty to come back with her.

Then she knew she had no means of compelling and
indeed no arguments to persuade Letty to do anything
she did not wish to do.

It was obvious that, if she had been wiser, she would
have seen that Letty was becoming more and more
dependent upon Sister Teresa.

In the last few days she no longer wished to be with
anyone else. She had not wanted Dorinda's company
or to talk to her as they had done when they had been
at home.

It was Sister Teresa with whom Letty felt comfortable
and on whom she relied for a feeling of safety and
security.

'It is hopeless!' Dorinda said. 'But how can I tell
him? How can I hurt him?'

She tossed and turned until it was nearly dawn and
then, because she was still very tired, she fell into a
fitful, restless sleep.

She woke and dressed early and went downstairs
feeling she must be prepared to see Maximus Kirby as
soon as he arrived so that he did not learn inadvertently
what had happened from anyone else.

There was always the danger that Lee Chang Lo
might tell him before she could reach him, so hoping
to ensure that this did not happen, she went to the
Secretary's office.

Lee Chang Lo rose as she entered, bowing courte-
ously, his hands ceremoniously crossed over each other
in the wide sleeves of his Chinese robe.

"You are better, Miss Hyde? I deeply regret to hear
that Mr. Kirby's life was in danger."

Dorinda was not surprised that he knew what had
happened.

The Doctor would have talked, and in a comparatively small and close-knit community such as Singapore anything that happened to Maximus Kirby was
sensational news.

"Dr. Seng did not wish Mr. Kirby to return until today," she replied. "When he arrives I wish to see him before anyone else speaks with him."

Lee Chang Lo bowed again.

"It shall be as you wish, Miss Hyde."

"Then please give those instructions to the servants."

"It shall be done, Miss Hyde."

She knew Lee Chang Lo understood. There was no need for her even to mention Letty or Sister Teresa.

His sharp brain would not have missed what she was trying to convey without her having to express it more clearly.

"I will wait for Mr. Kirby in the Library."

She thought that Maximus Kirby would arrive before luncheon, but she had to eat alone and then returned to the room filled with the books which she usually found so fascinating.

Now she knew that it would be impossible to read even one page and feel it could hold her attention.

She could only stand at the window looking out into the garden.

It seemed to her as if the sunshine was dim and she was encompassed about with darkness, dismay and apprehension.

How could she tell Maximus Kirby how sorry she was for what had happened? How could she excuse the fact that Letty had been foisted on him in the first place?

It was with a sense of relief that she realised that at least he did not know who she was.

To him she was only Letty's friend and companion, not the sister of the girl who had betrayed him.

It was as the sun was growing very hot and most people were taking a siesta that Dorinda heard through the open door the sound of horses' hoofs and wheels drawing up outside.

There was the noise of servants hurrying across the big room, then she heard Maximus Kirby's voice.

"Yes, I am quite all right, thank you. There was no need to worry about me. All is well."

One of the servants must have said that Dorinda was waiting for him, because she heard him say:

"Where is Miss Hyde?"

"In the Library, Sir."

"I will go to her."

And then as Dorinda felt as if her heart had stopped beating and it was impossible for her to breathe, there were his firm footsteps approaching the Library.

He seemed to fill the whole room.

Turning a white and frightened face towards him, Dorinda could only tremble at the thought of what she had to say.

Chapter Eight

When he saw Dorinda, Maximus Kirby came forward with a smile on his lips.

"I am back and I have so much to thank you . . ."

She put out her hand to stop him speaking.

He looked at her and asked quietly:

"What is the matter? What has upset you?"

It was incredibly difficult to find her voice but somehow she managed it.

"I have . . . something to . . . tell you."

"What is it?"

She thought the words would never pass her lips but at last she heard her own voice speaking and hardly recognized it.

"Letty has . . . gone away with . . . Sister Teresa!"

"Gone away?"

His tone was sharp.

"Sister Teresa has taken . . . Letty to . . . Sarawak . . . She is . . . sorry but she does not wish to . . . marry you. She left a note . . . asking me to tell . . . you so."

For a moment there was silence.

Dorinda could not look at Maximus Kirby; could not face the expression in his eyes, nor the anger she feared.

Then at last when she felt that she had waited for an incredibly long time, he exclaimed:

"Dammit, why did you not tell me the truth when I asked you?"

There was violence in his voice and Dorinda knew she could bear it no longer.

"I am . . . sorry," she whispered and ran from the room.

She did not know where she was going, she only knew she must get away. She could not face the questions with which she was sure Maximus Kirby would confront her.

She had almost forgotten that he had asked her on the yacht if Letty wished to marry him, and she had prevaricated making excuses for her sister.

Now she knew he would hate her for not being honest, for not preventing, as she could have done, this situation from arising.

Had she told the truth then, he could perhaps in some clever manner have prevented Letty from arriving in Singapore and saved himself the humiliation he must suffer now.

'Why was I . . . so stupid . . . so dishonest?' Dorinda asked herself.

Without being consciously aware of what she was doing, she had sought the sanctuary of her bed-room.

On an impulse, she picked up her hat and the handbag with which she had travelled and running downstairs again passed through the open door and out onto the steps.

A carriage was there as usual and seeing that she was waiting the coachman drew up under the portico.

"Go to the Shipping Office," she said.

As they travelled down the hill and through the streets, Dorinda was conscious of nothing but her own misery.

Now she knew that she must return home immediately—not only because she could not face Maximus Kirby's anger, but also because it would be impossible for her to stay in his house alone.

It was doubtful after what had happened if he would even speak to her, and yet, unimportant though he thought she was, she was still a young unmarried woman and the only possible thing she could do was to leave Singapore as soon as she could.

As she thought of what lay ahead Dorinda wanted to

cry out at the misery of it; to go on her knees if necessary to Maximus Kirby and ask him to let her stay.

Then she told herself that at least she had some pride left. She must behave like a lady, however reprehensible her sister's behaviour might appear.

She would return to England, forget that for one magical week she had been in the company of the man she loved, that for a very short time in her life she had been physically normal and looked like other girls of her age.

She was quite sure, whatever the Doctor had said, that once she was back in England her eczema would return.

Perhaps at first it would not be as bad as it had been before. But the cold of next winter would take its toll and then as winter after winter passed, she could become once again the ghost-like creature she had been before, creeping up the back-stairs of Alderburne Park, afraid of meeting people.

The carriage reached the Shipping Office without Dorinda having even noticed the streets through which they had passed.

She went inside and taking out her return ticket which she had kept in her hand-bag, she showed it to the Clerk.

"How soon will there be a Steam-Ship leaving for England?" she asked.

"The P. & O. liner *Homeric* will dock the day after tomorrow, Madam. It will arrive in the evening and leave the following morning."

"Will you please book me a cabin?"

"It will be a pleasure, Madam."

He made out a form in her name, and while she was waiting a man came into the office.

She did not even notice him until he exclaimed:

"Lady Dorinda! It is Lady Dorinda, isn't it?"

She looked round in surprise and saw the familiar face of a young man whom she had often met out hunting.

"I was not expecting to see you, Mr. Wakely!"

"Nor I you!" he replied. "Although I heard your sister had arrived in Singapore to marry Mr. Maximus Kirby, I didn't anticipate that you would be with her."

His eyes were searching her face and Dorinda knew, although he was too polite to say so, that he was astonished by her clear skin and the difference in her appearance.

"You look so well—I've never seen you look—so well!" he stammered.

"I am just arranging my return journey," Dorinda said, looking away a little shyly from the obvious admiration in his eyes.

"You can't be going back so soon? Why, you can have only just arrived."

"There are reasons why I must return to England."

She took the papers from the Clerk and thanked him.

"But I must see you, Lady Dorinda," Anthony Wakely said insistently. "But I had forgotten, you will be coming to the Ball tonight?"

"The Ball?" Dorinda queried.

"My sister is giving a Ball. You must have heard about it. I know that she sent an invitation to Lady Lettice and Mr. Kirby ten days ago."

"My sister has not been well."

"Well, if she cannot be present, you must!" Anthony Wakely said firmly, "and what is more, please say you will dine with us. I do not know whether you realize it, but my sister is married to Hugh Armstrong who owns a large plantation in Johore."

"No, I did not know!"

Vaguely Dorinda remembered hearing that one of the Wakely family lived out East. She had not thought to ask where.

"You will come tonight?" Anthony Wakely entreated as they left the Shipping Office and stood in the sunshine beside the carriage.

Suddenly Dorinda made up her mind to accept the invitation. Anything would be better than staying in Maximus Kirby's house and facing his anger.

There was tomorrow to go through before she could

leave Singapore and already she was wondering how she could endure it.

"I would like to come!" she said making up her mind. "Thank you for asking me."

"I will call for you at half-past seven," Anthony Wakely said. "If Lady Lettice and Mr. Kirby change their minds, my sister would of course be delighted to welcome them to dinner. But whatever happens, promise you'll not fail me?"

"I promise!" Dorinda said with a faint smile.

He helped her into the carriage, then stood bareheaded as she drove away.

He was a very presentable young man and as she well knew, an extremely good rider.

She had spoken to him more often than she had to other people out hunting simply because, like herself, he was usually in at the kill, and out-rode the rest of the field.

"I shall go to the Ball!" Dorinda told herself as the carriage brought her back to the house.

She felt it might be her last opportunity of ever being asked to such an occasion.

She was well aware that Anthony Wakely, though he was always very pleasant to her when out hunting, would never have invited her to a Ball in the past nor have asked her to dance with him at one.

It was vaguely comforting to know that at least one young man was ready to look at her with admiration in his eyes.

When she reached the house, she slipped upstairs to her bed-room.

There was no sign of Maximus Kirby and she was certain that having been away the day before he would have an enormous number of business matters to attend to, apart from the fact that she was sure he had no wish to see her.

She had tea upstairs, and then having taken a bath started to dress herself in good time so that she would be ready when Anthony Wakely arrived.

She brushed her hair in front of the mirror and saw

how buoyant and full of electricity it was. Now that it was thicker it waved softly over her shoulders and she could arrange it in any style she pleased.

On an impulse she swept it up on top of her head, pinning it into small curls in a fashion that gave her height and accentuated the long, graceful line of her neck.

She stared at herself seeing not the reflection of her shining head, but the lank, limp tresses with which she could do nothing when she was in England.

She rose to her feet.

'Just for tonight,' she thought, 'I will be Cinderella. I will go to the Ball looking, if not as beautiful as Letty, at least pretty and attractive. A girl with a clear, unblemished white skin. A woman with whom any man would be pleased to dance.'

She went from her own room into Letty's. She opened the wardrobe door. It was obvious that Letty had taken very little with her. Only the plainest, most simple gowns from her trousseau were missing.

Dorinda knew that Sister Teresa would have said that all the other more lovely creations which had come from Bond Street would be unsuitable and useless at a Mission in Sarawak.

Dorinda knew what was left only too well!

She had stood for hours fitting them; choosing the trimmings of satin, velvet and lace; making sure that the bodices fitted tightly, revealing the soft curves of the breasts and accentuating a tiny waist.

She reached out her hand almost defiantly and took from its hanger a dress of green crepe and tulle which she had liked more than any of the others.

The colour reminded her of the little green dragon that Maximus Kirby had given her. Then her mind shied away from thinking about him.

She slipped on the gown and turned to look at herself in the mirror.

It revealed every line of her perfect figure and frilled out below the knees into a train. Frills of tulle also cascaded down the back, held low down by a large bow of velvet ribbon.

She knew as she looked at herself that the green drew attention to the almost incredible whiteness of her skin, and seemed to pick up the lights in her eyes.

She looked quite different from the unobtrusive grey figure she had made herself out to be ever since she had left England, as Letty's Chaperon.

She remembered there was a small satin reticule to go with the gown and opened a drawer of the dressing-table.

Then she stared at what she saw.

Letty had taken with her none of the jewellery given to her by Maximus Kirby!

It was all lying loosely in the drawer, not even in boxes but tumbled together untidily in a glittering heap!

There was her engagement ring and the necklace and bracelet of sapphires which matched it. There were the pearls, the butterfly necklace, so colourful with its enamel ornamented with rubies, diamonds and emeralds.

Then Dorinda noticed something else.

It was a brooch she had known all her life. It was a crescent of diamonds which had been her mother's and which she sometimes lent to Letty to wear at parties.

It had been the Countess's wedding-present to her younger daughter.

"It would be stupid to spend money your father cannot afford on an expensive present," she had said to Letty. "So you had better have my diamond crescent."

"Thank you, Mama," Letty had murmured vaguely.

"You can always send it back, if Mr. Kirby loads you with jewels. I shall miss it."

'How could Letty have left it behind?' Dorinda asked.

Then she knew that diamonds given willingly or

grudgingly were not appropriate to the wilds of Sarawak.

'I had better take the brooch back to Mama,' Dorinda told herself and picked it up.

Then as she held it in her hand she looked down at it for a moment, and pinned it to the front of her dress.

She wondered what Maximus Kirby would do with all the jewellery that Letty had discarded. Would he sell it? Or would he keep it for the next woman he asked to become his wife?

At the thought of his being married Dorinda felt the pain she had experienced before stab her.

Then she asked herself despairingly what was the use of going on suffering? Once she had left Singapore it was doubtful if she would ever know what happened to him.

News of his marriage, or anything else he did, was hardly likely to reach Alderburne Park.

She shut the drawer of Letty's dressing-table and, having found the scarf which matched the gown and the reticule that went with it, she returned to her own bed-room.

She glanced at the clock. It was nearly half-past-seven. Walking on tip-toe she went to the head of the stairs.

There was no-one in the big room below except the servants. It was very quiet. There was only the sound of a clock ticking and the fragrance of flowers.

Dorinda waited.

Then after a few moments she heard the sound of an approaching carriage. She ran down the stairs as it drew up to the front door.

She had not been mistaken. It was Anthony Wakely calling to take her out to dinner.

She stepped into the carriage before he had time to alight.

"You've come!" he exclaimed. "I was afraid you might change your mind."

"I am looking forward to the Ball," Dorinda replied.

"And my sister is looking forward to meeting you," he said. "I told them how—well you are looking."

He stumbled over the words and Dorinda was well aware of what he had really said to his sister. But it did not matter. Tonight she wanted to hear every nice thing that could possibly be said about her appearance.

She wanted to be assured that she was pretty; that her gown became her; and to forget that in the future the cold winds and the sharp frosts would turn her back into a pitiful creature whom everyone avoided.

She was not really listening to what Anthony Wakely was saying to her except when he told her the Ball was to take place in the house that had once belonged to Sir Thomas Raffles.

"Oh, I had so hoped to see it!" Dorinda exclaimed.

"I cannot understand why Mr. Kirby has not taken you there," Anthony Wakely remarked. "It is one of the sights of Singapore."

Dorinda did not answer and he added:

"But of course, you told me that Lady Lettice has been ill. I am sorry. That means she will not be joining us tonight."

"I am afraid not."

"It is a pity. I told my brother-in-law and all their friends how beautiful she is, but I know they will not miss her when they see you!"

Dorinda smiled.

"You are flattering me!"

"I'm not!" he answered. "I had no idea that you were so pretty. Does that sound rude?"

He added the last words hastily as if afraid of offending her.

"I appreciate your compliment, Mr. Wakely," Dorinda said demurely.

The dinner-party, which was a very large one, would, Dorinda realised, have been an amusing experience had she not been conscious all the time of a dull ache within her breast that was almost like carrying a heavy stone about with her.

She tried not to think about Maximus Kirby, and

yet every breath she drew seemed somehow connected with him.

But she would not have been human if she had not realised that from the moment of her arrival at what was known as "The Raffles House" she was a success.

Anthony Wakely introduced her to everyone as proudly as if he was somehow responsible for her appearance, and the young Naval Officers from the ships, the Planters from the country and the Officials in the Government Offices fell over themselves to pay her compliments.

They clustered round Dorinda and stared at her with a wholehearted admiration which she had never known before.

She was vaguely aware that the girls and indeed some of the older women in the party were annoyed, but tonight their feelings did not matter.

'This is my Swan-Song,' she told herself. 'The day after tomorrow I shall be gone!'

The members of the dinner-party moved into the Ball-Room before the guests began to arrive and Anthony Wakely claimed the first dance.

It was exhilarating to be able to waltz, knowing she was light on her feet and that no-one was better dressed than she was.

It was even more exciting to find that partners were fighting amongst themselves to write their names down on her dance-card and even compiling a list when there were no more dances to give.

"Do you realise that you are the prettiest girl I have seen for years?"

"Why have I not seen you before?"

"Will you meet me tomorrow?"

"Please give me another dance?"

She answered the same questions over and over again, and yet because it was a new experience to her, there was something enthralling even about the repetition of them.

She went down to supper although she was not

hungry. Because of the ache in her breast she had been unable to eat at dinner.

She did however sip a little champagne and felt it brought her some escape from the thoughts and questions that kept encroaching upon her mind to spoil her enjoyment at being a success.

It was getting late and she was standing in the Ball-Room surrounded by half a dozen young men, waiting for the next dance to start when suddenly her eyes were drawn to the far end of the room.

She thought afterwards it must have been instinct rather than anything else that made her look towards the entrance.

Then she saw him!

He walked onto the floor seeming taller, more broad-shouldered and more dominating in personality than any other man in the room.

It was as if he dwarfed everybody else.

Then, as if some magnetism passing between them made him find her instantly, Maximus Kirby came towards Dorinda.

She stood watching him and for a moment the voices and the laughter of the men surrounding her faded away into nothing. She could not hear them and she was hardly conscious that they were there.

As he reached her side Anthony Wakely saw him.

"Mr. Kirby. I am so glad you could come after all!" he exclaimed. "It has been marvellous for us to be able to entertain Lady Dorinda, but we did miss you and Lady Lettice."

Dorinda felt as if she was turned to stone. She knew that for a moment Maximus Kirby was also very still.

He did not answer Anthony Wakely, he did not even look at him. His eyes were on Dorinda's face. Then as the music started, he stepped forward and put his arm round her.

"This is our dance," he said.

Before Dorinda's promised partner could speak, he swept her onto the dance floor.

She was vividly conscious of his arm holding her, of her hand in his.

But she did not dare look at him, and it would have been impossible even if her life had depended on it, for her to speak.

The floor was crowded but Maximus Kirby moved skilfully between the dancers until they reached the far end of the room where there were long windows opening onto a verandah.

Maximus Kirby stopped dancing and taking Dorinda by the arm drew her firmly from the Ball-Room and out into the garden.

She wanted to protest. She wanted to say she could not go with him. But she felt utterly helpless and knew that in actual fact she had no choice but to obey whatever he asked of her.

They walked across the smooth lawn to the far end of it where they were sheltered from the house by some flowering shrubs.

Maximus Kirby stopped in the light of a lantern half-hidden by the flowering branches of a tree.

Then he took his hand from her arm and faced her.

"*Lady* Dorinda!" he said, stressing the title, "and so this is another way in which you have deceived me!"

"I came . . . out . . . as Letty's . . . companion," Dorinda said in a low voice, "because we . . . thought it might be . . . embarrassing for me to be known as her . . . sister."

"Embarrassing?"

The word sounded jeering on Maximus Kirby's lips.

"So you are part of the plot to foist a half-witted, immature child upon me as my wife!"

"It was . . . not like . . . that."

"I see now exactly what happened," he went on. "I understand how much your father wanted a rich son-in-law, and how easily I stepped into the trap he set for me."

There was so much contempt in his tone that Dorinda found herself trembling.

"He did . . . not mean to deceive . . . you."

"You are lying! Again you are lying, and you, like your parents and your sister, have contrived to make me look a complete fool."

"I . . . I am . . . sorry," Dorinda faltered, "desperately . . . sorry."

"Do you think that is enough?" Maximus Kirby asked, "for holding me up to ridicule and making me a laughing-stock in front of my friends and employees?"

The harshness in his voice made her cry desperately:

"How can I . . . explain? What can I . . . do?"

He looked down at her and she thought in the light of the lantern the expression on his face was cruel.

"I will tell you what you can do. One daughter of an Earl is very much like another. You will marry me! You came to Singapore to see me married. Well, I would not wish you to be disappointed! You can take your sister's place!"

Then as Dorinda stared at him wide-eyed, too shocked and astonished even to comprehend what he was saying, he pulled her so roughly into his arms that she gave a little cry.

He held her so that she could hardly breathe and then he tipped back her head and his lips were on hers.

For a moment she was only conscious that he hurt her almost unbearably, that his mouth was brutal, bruising the softness of her lips.

Then as it seemed to her he held her even closer, his kiss was different, more compelling, more insistent, more demanding.

She wanted to thrust him away from her, to fight for her freedom.

Instead she felt a weakness like a warm wave creeping up her body and into her throat.

It was so insidious, so inescapable that she could feel herself go limp in his arms and surrender her own mouth to his.

His lips grew more gentle and now Dorinda knew a sudden wonder and rapture such as she had never believed possible.

It was something so magical and entrancing that she felt as if he drew her very heart from her body.

Then as she thought he was about to take his mouth from hers, he twisted the softness of her lips with his and she felt a thrill like a streak of forked-lightning seep through her body.

For a moment it was only a dagger-like pain, then it was an ecstasy beyond belief; a wonder that made her quiver and tremble because of its intensity.

She had not known it was possible to have such feelings until even as she tried to hold the rapture of it, to know it was the most perfect thing that had ever happened to her, Maximus Kirby raised his head and she was free.

He was about to speak; perhaps to curse or scold her or to jeer at her as he had done already.

But Dorinda knew she could not bear it; could not listen to his anger and contempt; to his denunciation of her deception after that moment which had been, for the second it lasted, a part of Heaven itself.

With a little cry and a strength she did not know she possessed, she fought herself free of his arms and picking up her skirts ran across the garden, moving so swiftly that she was almost out of sight before he realised what had happened.

Using some instinct of self-preservation, Dorinda avoided the Ball-Room and slipped down a passageway which led to the front door.

She stood breathlessly on the steps looking for a conveyance.

"Carriage, Madam?" a Linkman asked.

"Yes . . . please," Dorinda replied with difficulty.

A carriage appeared and she stepped into it.

"Where to, Madam?"

"The Quay."

The coachman whipped up the tired horse and as they started off Dorinda looked back.

There was no sign of Maximus Kirby amongst a number of people leaving the house.

She put her hands up to her face. Now she knew that she could not meet him again.

He loathed and despised her, but she loved him to the point when she could not trust herself not to break down and tell him so.

He had undoubtedly been in a furious rage when he had spoken of marrying her but, even if he repeated such an outrageous suggestion the next day, she knew there was nothing she could do but refuse him.

It would be an unbearable crucifixion to know he was marrying her to save his pride and that he hated her because she had been part of the plot to deceive him.

In everything he had ever attempted Maximus Kirby had been overwhelmingly successful except in his plans for his marriage. Would he ever forgive, or even tolerate, a woman who thoughtlessly, inadvertently, had been part of his only failure?

She loved him too much. He evoked feelings within her she could not control and there was nothing she could do except put an ocean between them.

'I cannot see him again . . . I cannot!' Dorinda told herself.

The carriage came to a stand-still and she looked out onto the Quay and saw many ships' lights, green and red, reflected on the sea beneath them.

Dorinda was sure some Booking-Office would be open because many ships sailed at dawn.

She told the carriage to wait and walking across the pavement found, as she had expected, a small office plastered with advertisements of Steam Ship Lines with long lists of future sailings.

She did not wait to read them but asked the Chinese clerk when the next ship would be leaving Port.

"There is one leaving within five minutes," he replied. "It is a cargo vessel but it also carries passengers."

"Where is it going?" Dorinda asked.

"To Djakarta," he answered.

For a moment Dorinda could not even remember where it was, but it did not matter.

"I want a first class cabin."

"There is only one cabin aboard," the Clerk answered, "and it is empty."

He made out a ticket, apparently not in the least interested in her appearance or the fact that ladies in evening gowns did not usually wish to sail on cargo ships.

Dorinda opened her reticule, then saw to her consternation she had no money with her.

For a moment she felt frightened that she would not be able to get away until she remembered the diamond crescent she wore in the front of her gown.

She unclasped it and set it down on the counter in front of the Clerk.

"It is valuable," she said, "I want whatever money you can get for it to take with me."

His imperturbable Eastern face was quite expressionless. He picked up the brooch and after holding it close to the oil-lamp which flickered beside him, he knocked on the back of the office.

For a moment there was no movement, then a very old Chinaman with a long, grey beard came out.

The two men exchanged about half-a-dozen words. The old man peered at the brooch, examined it with a magnifying glass and went back into the room from which he had come.

Dorinda realised that this sort of thing must often have happened before. Barter was something the Chinese understood. Goods, whatever they might be, would always fetch money.

The old man came back into the office and said something to the Clerk who translated it to Dorinda.

"The brooch is worth one hundred and fifty pounds. We will give you eighty."

"I will take it!" Dorinda replied.

She felt she should have argued, but she had only one urgent desire, to leave Singapore on the ship that was sailing in a few minutes.

The Clerk deducted the price of the ticket. She took

the money, paid off the carriage, stuffed the rest into her reticule and then ran down the Quay.

It was still night but even as she reached the ship the first golden fingers of dawn appeared in the East and the darkness receded.

The ship was small and squalid with only two decks, the lower one crowded with poor Chinese and Malayans, all herded together amongst the cargo of boxes and bales, animals and chickens in coops.

There was, however, a separate gang-plank that led to the upper deck. It was steep and Dorinda picked up her dress so that she would not trip over her green tulle frills.

A Chinese sailor showed her into the cabin, which was close to the funnel and later would be, she thought, excessively hot.

It did not matter!

She was getting away and the fact that the bare cabin, with its two hard bunks, a chair and a table, was like a prison cell was of no consequence.

The sailor shut the door behind her and she walked the few feet across the dirty wooden floor to stand at the port-hole looking out at the harbour.

Now the sun was rising to shimmer on the smooth sea, to flood the whole world with a golden radiance.

Looking at Singapore through the thick glass of the port-hole, Dorinda felt that this was the last glimpse she would have of everything that had ever mattered to her.

But she was no longer a part of it. She was leaving behind not only her heart but her whole soul.

She felt the tears come into her eyes and then the memory of what she had felt when Maximus Kirby had kissed her seemed to sear through her body like a flame.

Nothing could have been so utterly and unbearably marvellous, and yet because it was a wonder beyond words, she could not let herself be destroyed by his anger.

'I love you!' she whispered aloud looking out onto

the sun-lit sea. 'I love you . . . but I could not endure
your . . . hatred and . . . live!'

She heard the ship's bell ring and there was a sudden
hoot from the funnel. The engines started up and began
to shake the whole cabin.

She was leaving. And now she could no longer see
through her tears.

'Good-bye, my love!' she whispered and hid her face
in her hands.

There was a sudden crash so loud, so unexpected
that Dorinda jumped and turned round sharply.

Standing in the doorway of the cabin was Maximus
Kirby!

For a moment she could only stare at him. Then
without speaking he reached out, took her by the wrist,
pulled her through the door-way and out onto the deck.

The ship was moving, the gang-way on the top deck
had gone and a sailor was ready to replace the break
in the ship's rail where it had stood.

Without speaking and so quickly that Dorinda did
not anticipate what was to happen, Maximus Kirby
picked her up in his arms and holding her tightly against
his breast, he jumped!

The ship was already clear of the Quayside. There
was a drop of five feet, but he landed on his feet.
Dorinda gasping felt as if all the breath had been
knocked out of her body.

It had all happened before she could even realise
what he was doing.

Then, as she hid her face against his shoulder, fighting to breathe and jarred by the impact when they had
touched the ground, she could hear the people on the
ship and those on the Quayside cheering and clapping
their hands.

She had the idea that Maximus Kirby was smiling as
he walked away down the Quay still holding her in his
arms.

He passed the Booking Office and went to where his
open carriage was waiting.

It was drawn by two horses. Dorinda realised why he

had been able to overtake her but at the same time she wondered why he had bothered to do so.

The tears were still wet on her lashes and on her cheeks. Without a word Maximus Kirby set her down in a corner of the carriage, drew his handkerchief from his breast-pocket and wiped her face.

His action was so gentle that she felt the tears start into her eyes again, and taking the handkerchief from him she hid her face in it, crying, because she was unable to stop herself.

"Why did you not let me go?" she wanted to ask him.

But it was impossible to say anything at the moment, not only because of her tears, but because she was still breathless.

'How could he have risked breaking a leg in such a manner?' she wondered, and knew it was because he was determined to have his own way, even where she was concerned.

'I must . . . talk to him . . . I must . . . make him . . . understand,' she thought frantically.

At the same time she was not quite certain of what she wanted him to understand or how she could find an excuse for what had happened.

They had hardly travelled any distance when the horses came to a stand-still. Wonderingly, Dorinda took the handkerchief from her eyes.

For a moment she thought they had not in fact moved. They were still at the harbour and then she saw beside a small jetty there were two yachts.

One was *The Sea Dragon* on which they had travelled the previous week, gleaming with white paint, very spic and span in the sun-light, and near her was the most fantastic ship Dorinda had ever seen.

A huge Chinese junk, twice the size of those she had seen as they came down the Coast, it was painted red and gold and there was the carved figure-head of a mermaid on the bow.

As she stared at it Maximus Kirby alighted from his side of the carriage and came round to hers.

He opened the door.

"Will you walk, or shall I carry you?"

It was the first time he had spoken since he had raged at her in the garden before he kissed her.

She looked at him for a moment, her eyes wide, puzzled and frightened. Then the expression on his face made her heart start beating frantically.

She looked into his grey eyes and something seemed to pass between them; something she did not understand and dared not put into words.

He helped her to the ground and they walked the short distance to *The Sea Nymph*. He assisted her aboard.

An Officer wearing the uniform of a First Mate saluted them.

"Welcome aboard, Sir."

"Put to sea, Mr. Chang," Maximus Kirby replied, "and ask Captain Barnet to come to the Saloon immediately."

"Aye, aye, Sir."

Maximus Kirby guided Dorinda below and she found herself in a large Saloon which ran the whole length of the ship.

There were huge sofas, deep chairs and surprisingly vases of flowers beside a bookcase filled with books and a desk against one wall.

Dorinda only had a quick impression before she turned her face towards Maximus Kirby. She was very pale and there was a question in her eyes.

For a moment they looked at each other. Then in a trembling voice she asked:

"Why have . . . you brought . . . me here?"

Chapter Nine

Dorinda knew that Maximus Kirby was feeling for words, but before he could speak the door of the Saloon opened and Captain Barnet entered.

He was a middle-aged man, and even without his uniform one would have known from his sun-burnt face and pale blue eyes that he was a sailor.

"It's good to see you, Mr. Kirby," the Captain said as he advanced.

Maximus Kirby shook hands with him, then to Dorinda:

"I would like to introduce Captain Barnet, the trusted Commander of *The Sea Nymph* and the other ships of my small fleet."

"Which grows bigger every day!" the Captain added with a smile.

He bowed politely to Dorinda.

"Honoured to have you aboard, Ma'am."

"And now, Captain Barnet," Maximus Kirby said. "Lady Dorinda and I will be obliged if you would marry us!"

Dorinda looked at Maximus Kirby in sheer astonishment.

For a moment no-one spoke, and then the Captain calmly, as if such a request was by no means unusual, replied:

"Certainly, Sir. I believe there is a prayerbook in the book-case."

He crossed the Saloon as he spoke.

Dorinda stood staring at Maximus Kirby, feeling she had either been mistaken in what she heard, or that it was some peculiar jest.

But Maximus Kirby's grey eyes were very serious as they looked into hers, and she had the strangest feeling that he was telling her something which she did not understand.

She wanted to protest, to argue with him. But she knew she could not do so in front of the Captain.

Maximus Kirby had already been humiliated enough by the way in which Letty had behaved. It would be as bad, if not worse, if she queried his authority in front of a man he employed.

She wanted to beg of him not to go any further with what she was certain was his idea of revenge—a way of getting his own back because he had been tricked by her father.

As she thought frantically she must ask to speak with him alone, the Captain returned to their side, a prayer-book in his hand.

"I have found it, Sir, if you are ready," he said taking off his cap and laying it on a side-table.

"No! No! You cannot do this!" Dorinda wished to say, but when Maximus Kirby held out his hand the words died on her lips and because she felt too helpless to defy him, she obediently placed her hand in his.

She felt the hard strength of his fingers and knew that he must be aware that she trembled.

"We are ready, Captain Barnet," Maximus Kirby said in his deep voice.

As the Captain started to read the Marriage Service, Dorinda felt that her will had gone, that she was no longer herself but utterly subservient to the man beside her.

Maximus Kirby made every response in a firm tone while to Dorinda her own voice sounded weak and frightened.

When they had taken their Marriage Vows, Maximus Kirby drew off his signet-ring and put it on the third finger of Dorinda's left hand. It was a plain gold ring with a small flat emerald in the centre of it bearing his initials.

As if in a dream she heard him say slowly:

"With this ring, I thee wed. With my body I thee worship. With all my worldly goods I thee endow."

It could not be true! It must be her imagination! She could not be listening to words which joined her to the man she loved for life—for all time.

Captain Barnet cleared his throat and said impressively:

"With the authority vested in me as a Ship's Captain by Her Britannic Majesty, Queen Victoria, Empress of India, I now pronounce you man and wife, and may the Lord God bless your union."

He closed the prayer-book.

Maximus Kirby did not relinquish Dorinda's hand, but raised it to his lips. She felt his mouth against her skin and for no reason that she could explain, she wanted to cry.

"My best congratulations, Sir," Captain Barnet said, "and you too, Lady Dorinda. I hope you will have many years of happiness together."

He took his cap from the side-table, placed it on his head, saluted smartly and left the Saloon.

Dorinda drew her hand away from Maximus Kirby's. The signet-ring was too big for her and she put her other hand over it to prevent it slipping off.

Then she looked up at him, her eyes dark and troubled.

"Are we . . . really . . . married?"

She could hardly breathe the words.

"We are married according to the Law of England," Maximus Kirby replied. "You are my wife, Dorinda."

Her eyes dropped before his.

"You have . . . made a . . . mistake," she said miserably.

She expected him to answer her, but instead he drew his watch from his waist-coat pocket.

"It is now a little after four o'clock in the morning. I think you must be tired, so I suggest you go to bed.

There will be plenty of time for us to talk over what has occurred later in the day."

As he spoke he walked across the cabin to open a door in the other wall.

Almost automatically Dorinda followed him. The front of the junk appeared to have been divided into two parts, one being the Saloon, the other the bed-room.

It was very large for a ship and in the centre was the strangest bed Dorinda had ever seen.

It was ornamented at the back and foot with carved gilt dragons and flowers against a background of the same soft green piece of jade which Maximus Kirby had given her.

The whole cabin was green: the carpet, the walls, the bed covering and the silk curtains which covered the port-holes. It was cool and exquisite giving almost an impression of being under-water.

Dorinda stared in bewilderment.

Then Maximus Kirby said:

"Go to sleep, Dorinda. Everything will seem less alarming when you wake."

He went from the cabin as he spoke and shut the door behind him.

Dorinda stood still in the cool, green dimness which was like a mermaid's cave. Then almost automatically, because he had told her to do so, she began to unfasten her gown.

She saw there was a wardrobe against one wall and walked to it to hang her dress inside. She opened the doors to stand transfixed!

It was filled with dresses which she immediately recognized.

All of them were the gowns that she had looked at only a few hours ago in Letty's bed-room; the gowns she had fitted in London because her sister refused to do so. Then she understood!

It was only another example of Maximus Kirby's efficiency. Just as Lee Chang Lo had told her, his own clothes were duplicated on his yachts, so Chinese tailors had copied Letty's.

Dorinda hung up her gown, shut the doors of the wardrobe, and then found a variety of nightgowns, also copied from Letty's, in a drawer of a chest.

It was painted with flowers and long tailed phoenixes, besides being carved and gilded Chinese-fashion, at every corner.

Dorinda put on a very thin muslin nightgown and got into bed.

As she did so she looked apprehensively at the closed door. Would Maximus Kirby come to her . . . as her . . . husband?

She felt tense and worried. There was so much she wished to tell him. So much she had to try and explain. But he had been right in saying she was tired. The bed was so comfortable, the pillows were soft.

She lay looking at the door and did not know the moment she fell asleep . . .

There was the sound of water, the soft slap of the wind in a sail, and again the cool ripple of small waves against a wooden prow.

Dorinda lay listening for a little while, not fully aware of where she was. Then in a sudden fright she remembered.

She was married and she was aboard "The Sea Nymph"! It had not been a dream.

She sat up in bed, the green cabin was cool and dim. The door was open and through it she could see the Saloon.

On a big sofa opposite the door which led into her cabin she could see Maximus Kirby. He was lying stretched out on a sofa and he was fast asleep!

Dorinda sat up looking at him for some time. Then she lay down again . . .

She awoke conscious of someone's presence. She opened her eyes and saw that Maximus Kirby was standing beside her.

"I have brought you a cup of tea," he said in his deep voice.

She looked up at him sleepily.

She had been dreaming of him and she felt an irrepressible happiness sweep over her because he was actually there.

Then she remembered what had happened the night before!

He sat down on the bed facing her and she took the handleless cup of China tea from him.

It was hot and fragrant. As she sipped it she looked at him.

Her hair waved as it fell over her shoulders, there was a faint flush in her cheeks and her eyes were still a little hazy with sleep. Maximus Kirby thought he had never known a woman so unselfconscious about her appearance.

Dorinda saw that he was wearing a silk scarf round his neck and a blue cotton gown which reached to the ground.

His hair looked damp.

"I have been swimming," he explained as if in answer to a question she had not put into words.

"It sounds . . . lovely . . . but was it safe?"

Maximus Kirby smiled.

"The sailors kept watch for sharks, but if I had been in danger I am sure you would somehow have saved me."

Dorinda smiled shyly. He took the empty cup from her and set it down on a table which stood by the bed.

"I think we have a lot to say to each other, Dorinda."

She pressed herself back a little against the pillows as if they fortified her against a sudden weakness.

"But before we start," he went on, "I want you to tell me why you said our marriage was a mistake."

Dorinda drew in her breath.

There were so many reasons she could give him, she thought. Then she said the first that came into her mind.

"I am not . . . pretty . . . enough!"

Maximus Kirby smiled.

"That is a very feminine reason," he said softly.

He reached out his hand, put his fingers under her chin and lifted her face up.

"Perhaps I should have told you before that you are the most beautiful person I have ever seen in my whole life!"

He felt Dorinda stiffen and look at him incredulously, as if she thought he was making fun of her.

"It is quite true! You are like my Chinese paintings. It is what lies behind your worried eyes, your adorable little nose and your soft lips which entrances and enthralls me and holds me spell-bound until I can never cease looking not only at your beauty but at the loveliness beneath it."

Dorinda quivered at the depth of feeling in his voice.

"Are you . . . telling me the . . . truth?"

"Do you really think I would lie to you about something which concerns us both so deeply?"

He saw the shadow of disbelief still in her eyes and went on:

"Perhaps you are wondering, my darling, why I have married you as I have, without any spectators, without white horses, doves, fountains or fire-works?"

He paused and asked:

"Tell me why do you think I wanted none of those things?"

He obviously expected an answer and after what seemed a long silence Dorinda said hesitatingly:

"I suppose . . . because you were . . . not proud of me . . . as you . . . would have been of . . Letty."

Maximus Kirby made a movement as if he would have taken her in his arms, but he checked himself and only laid his hand on hers.

"The reason was that neither you nor I need that sort of ostentation. Do you imagine that I would parade my precious treasures before those who would not understand them?"

His fingers tightened over hers and he said:

"I want you to believe me when I tell you that you are the only woman and the only European who has ever entered the secret rooms in the old part of my house to look at my pictures. I have many more that I am waiting to show you, and you—alone."

Dorinda felt as though something magnetic and vibrant passed from his hand to hers and now in a voice so low he could hardly hear she stammered:

"Are you . . . s . saying that you . . . c . care . . . for me?"

"I love you! I have loved you since the first moment we met. I knew it when we talked together after I had kissed that Planter's importunate wife and you told me I was generous with my kisses!"

He smiled.

"I knew then that you were different from any other woman I have ever known. Then when you behaved so bravely when the pirates attacked us and when I talked to you as we sailed down the Coast, I was aware that something very strange had happened to me."

He was silent for a moment before he continued:

"It is difficult to make you understand, my lovely one, but I have never really talked with a woman before."

Dorinda's eyes were on his and he went on:

"Women have always seemed to me like Birds of Paradise. I have desired them, been infatuated, captivated, amused by them, but—and this may seem brutal to you—they were easily dispensable."

Dorinda thought of "Perfect Pearl" and "Goldie." They had certainly been Birds of Paradise in his life!

"I have never known a woman until I met you," he went on, "with whom I wished to discuss my business matters; who could be a part not only of my heart but of my life."

"How did you . . . know that I was . . . different?"

"My instinct has never failed me. That first night it told me you should stay in Singapore—with me!"

He gave a deep sigh.

"After that I showed you my pictures. I could not explain even to myself why I broke my golden rule and took you to a part of the house where no other woman has ever been."

"What did you . . . think then?"

"I was afraid."

"Afraid?"

"Yes, because I knew that something had happened to me which had never happened before."

"What was that?"

"I had fallen deeply and irrevocably in love!"

"Can . . . that really be . . . true?"

"That is exactly what I asked myself! I could not believe it, I could hardly credit that what I was feeling was not just a passionate desire because you were so lovely, but something very different—a yearning which was a spiritual need."

"And yet you . . . never talked to me . . . alone again."

"I told you I was afraid—afraid of the future, unsure of myself perhaps for the first time in my life, and completely without a solution to the problem of what to do either about Letty or about you."

"I had no idea . . . that you even . . . thought about me."

"How could I know if you cared for me?"

He took her hand between both of his and looked down at it.

"Such a small hand, and yet I knew when I watched you at the table talking so intelligently and brilliantly to my friends that my whole happiness was in your keeping."

"If . . . only you had . . . told me."

"Would that have solved anything?" he asked. "I used to lie awake night after night wondering how I could explain to Letty that I could not marry her, striving desperately to find a way out of the trap I had set for myself and from which there seemed no honourable escape."

"I can understand . . . you felt like . . . that."

"Then you saved my life when the viper bit me," he continued, "and yesterday as I drove back to Singapore I thought that perhaps by some miracle you must love me a little to have risked your life for mine."

"A . . . little!" Dorinda murmured almost with a sob,

remembering how much she had suffered when she thought he might die.

"When I reached home you told me that Letty had gone with Sister Teresa."

"But you were angry . . . you were angry with me!"

"Only because you had lied to me. I had believed you to be honest, so utterly without guile. I had not thought for a moment you were concerned in what I now realised had been a plot to marry me to a child who had never grown up."

Dorinda's eyes dropped before this. She was ashamed when she thought of the ten thousand pounds her father had taken from him.

"But I was glad with an inexpressible gladness that I was free!" he went on. "Now I could ask you to become my wife! But because I felt I must show some sort of propriety and decorum I did not approach you last night, but I certainly did not expect that you would have gone to a Ball with another man!"

His fingers tightened on hers until they hurt.

"When I learnt late in the evening that you were not upstairs asleep, as I had imagined, but at a party, I was consumed by an emotion which again was one I have never felt before—jealousy!"

He gave a wry smile.

"I have often laughed in the past at men who were jealous of their women. I know now that the reason I had been immune is that I had never been in love."

The note in his voice made Dorinda thrill, and she remembered how jealous she had been of him.

"When I saw you standing in the Ball-Room surrounded by men, I wanted for the first time in my life to commit murder in cold blood! You looked unbelievably lovely, but at that moment I also wanted to hurt you. I was everything that is primitive; a man ready to drag the woman who belonged to him away into a cave and beat her into submission."

He gave a short laugh.

"You are fortunate, my precious, that I offered you nothing more violent than a kiss!"

The colour rose in Dorinda's cheeks as she remembered what the kiss had meant to her.

As if he understood, Maximus Kirby said:

"But when I kissed your lips I realised two things."

"What were . . . they?"

"First that you had never been kissed before, and secondly that you loved me!"

Now the colour in Dorinda's cheeks rose in a crimson tide, and once again he raised her chin so that he could look into her face.

"It is true? You do love me? I was not mistaken?"

"I love . . . you!" Dorinda managed to whisper although she was trembling.

Then when she thought his lips might seek hers, she added quickly:

"Please . . . there is something . . . I must . . . tell you."

He took his hand away and waited.

She could not look at him. Her head was bowed, her eye-lashes very long and dark.

She could not think for a moment how to put into words what she wished to say.

"I am waiting," Maximus said gently.

"I do not . . . know how to tell . . . you."

"Shall we make it a little easier and a great deal more comfortable?" he suggested.

He rose as he spoke to turn round and lie down on the bed beside her, his back against the pillows. He raised his feet onto the light green cover under which Dorinda had slept.

He put his arm behind her and drew her close against him. He felt the quiver that went through her whole body and he said quietly:

"You will find it easier like this my sweet, to tell me what has to be said, however difficult it may be."

It was indeed easier, Dorinda thought. His arm gave her a feeling of security and in some strange way she was no longer afraid.

"When you came to Alderburne Park," she began in a very small voice, "the reason you did not meet me was that I was so . . . ugly! I never appeared when there were guests because they would have been . . . disgusted by my . . . appearance."

"What was wrong?"

She knew whatever he had expected to hear, it was certainly not this!

"I had a skin complaint and none of the Doctors in England could do anything to cure it. It . . . disfigured me and because of it people never looked at me . . . directly."

There was a little throb in her voice which told the man listening how much she must have suffered.

"You can guess however," she went on, "that the only reason I came out to Singapore with Letty was that she could not have gone without . . . me. Papa and I knew that even if we could . . . persuade her to start out on the voyage, it was unlikely that she would . . . agree to . . . marry you . . . once she . . . arrived."

Dorinda's voice was very faint. She knew she implicated herself in her father's plot, but she had to be honest.

"Go on," Maximus Kirby said.

"When we reached the Red Sea, a miracle happened. I awoke one morning to find the eczema had gone and my skin was clear!"

"I have heard of that happening."

"Doctor Johnson said it will not return unless I go back to live in the cold, dry climate of England."

"That makes things very simple, does it not? Is that all you have to tell me?"

"There is . . . something . . . else."

"What is it?"

She turned her face against his shoulder.

"You said," she whispered, "that you have liked . . . talking to me; that you think I am . . . clever and intelligent. But because I was so . . . ugly, I know nothing about . . . men or about . . . love . . . I am afraid that I shall . . . bore you."

Maximus Kirby took his arm away from Dorinda and

as she slipped back against the pillows he turned round to look down at her.

"Do you really think that I want you to know anything about other men or to let anyone teach you about love except me?"

His lips tightened for a moment.

"I will kill any man who ever touches you! You are mine!"

Dorinda drew in her breath at the violence with which he spoke. Then he went on:

"You are everything, my precious heart, I wanted to find in a woman, everything I have longed for, searched for, and did not believe existed except in my own imagination."

"Is that . . . true?"

"It is something I shall have to prove so that you will believe me."

His voice was very deep.

He bent forward and now his lips were very near to hers.

"I love you! I love you beyond words and at last I have found a wife who is mine, all mine, yet she possesses my heart and my soul."

His mouth found hers. Dorinda felt that strange streak that was both pain and pleasure run through her body like a flame.

He held her closer and closer still, until she could no longer think but only feel in a wild uncontrollable ecstasy that they were one . . .

There was only the sound of the water splashing against the wooden hull and the wind moving faintly in the sails overhead.

"Do you still . . . love me?" a little voice whispered.

Maximus Kirby drew Dorinda's body close against his. It was very soft and yielding.

"That is the question I should ask you, my darling."

"I did not . . . disappoint you?"

"My precious, do I really need to tell you it was the

most wonderful, most perfect, most supreme moment of my life?"

Dorinda gave a little sigh.

"I did not . . . know that . . . love was like . . . that!"

"Like what?"

"Like a fire, or perhaps lightning. I always thought it would be warm and quiet, gentle and cosy, not something so . . . intense that it is almost too . . . painful and yet a rapture."

He smiled and kissed her forehead.

"You have described it well. It was what the Chinese call 'the knife-edge of ultimate joy'."

"That is exactly what it is."

She gave a little cry.

"Oh, Max! I know now . . ."

"Know what, my sweet?"

"What your picture means . . . the one I could not understand."

"Tell me."

"The two streams that join each other under the bridge are man and woman linked by marriage. The clouds are the ceiling of ordinary life, the day-to-day world in which we live. But the white peaks above, vivid against the sky, are the ecstasy which we find . . . together when we make . . . love."

Maximus Kirby turned sideways to look down at his wife.

"Is that what I make you feel?"

"You . . . know you . . . do."

"Oh, my perfect darling, that is what I have wanted; what I have prayed for."

"I love you until it is an . . . agony and yet an unbelievable . . . glory all in one."

There was a radiance in Dorinda's eyes that was like a light and her skin even in the dimness of the green room looked translucent like a pearl as it comes from the sea.

"Do you still think our marriage was a mistake?" he asked.

"No . . . no . . . it is . . . magnificent."

He looked at her for a long moment and she thought he was about to kiss her mouth, but he moved his lips along first one of her eyebrows and then the other.

He kissed her eyes, her small ears, then the round softness of her neck, evoking strange feelings she had never felt before.

"I love . . . you!" she whispered, her breath coming fitfully between her lips. "I love . . . you . . . my wonderful . . . magnificent . . . husband . . ."

His kisses became more insistent and her body moved beneath his.

His mouth asked the absolute and complete surrender of herself. His lips were passionate and fiercely demanding.

Then there were only the mountain peaks and the "knife-edge of ultimate joy."

ABOUT THE AUTHOR

BARBARA CARTLAND, the celebrated romantic author, historian, playwright, lecturer, political speaker and television personality, has now written over 150 books. Miss Cartland has had a number of historical books published and several biographical ones, including that of her brother, Major Ronald Cartland, who was the first Member of Parliament to be killed in the War. This book had a Foreword by Sir Winston Churchill.

In private life, Barbara Cartland, who is a Dame of the Order of St. John of Jerusalem, has fought for better conditions and salaries for Midwives and Nurses. As President of the Royal College of Midwives (Hertfordshire Branch), she has been invested with the first Badge of Office ever given in Great Britain, which was subscribed to by the Midwives themselves. She has also championed the cause for old people and founded the first Romany Gypsy Camp in the world.

Barbara Cartland is deeply interested in Vitamin Therapy and is President of the British National Association for Health.

Barbara Cartland

The world's bestselling author of romantic fiction.
Her stories are always captivating tales of intrigue,
adventure and love.

☐	THE BORED BRIDEGROOM	6381	$1.25
☐	THE PENNILESS PEER	6387	$1.25
☐	CASTLE OF FEAR	8103	$1.25
☐	THE GLITTERING LIGHTS	8104	$1.25
☐	A SWORD TO THE HEART	8105	$1.25
☐	THE KARMA OF LOVE	8106	$1.25
☐	THE MAGNIFICENT MARRIAGE	8166	$1.25
☐	THE RUTHLESS RAKE	8240	$1.25
☐	LESSONS IN LOVE	8261	95¢
☐	THE DARING DECEPTION	8265	95¢
☐	NO DARKNESS FOR LOVE	8275	95¢
☐	THE LITTLE ADVENTURE	8278	95¢
☐	THE DANGEROUS DANDY	8280	$1.25
☐	JOURNEY TO PARADISE	8362	95¢
☐	THE WICKED MARQUIS	8467	$1.25

Buy them at your local bookseller or use this handy coupon:

Bantam Books, Inc., Dept. BC, 414 East Golf Road, Des Plaines, Ill. 60016

Please send me the books I have checked above. I am enclosing $_____
(please add 35¢ to cover postage and handling). Send check or money order
—no cash or C.O.D.'s please.

Mr/Mrs/Miss_____

Address_____

City_____State/Zip_____

BC—2/75

Please allow three weeks for delivery. This offer expires 2/76.

Bantam Book Catalog

It lists over a thousand money-saving bestsellers originally priced from $3.75 to $15.00 —bestsellers that are yours now for as little as 50¢ to $2.95!

The catalog gives you a great opportunity to build your own private library at huge savings!

So don't delay any longer—send us your name and address and 10¢ (to help defray postage and handling costs).